LLEYELLYN

A N O V E L

Ross A. Phelps

ISBN 978-0-9903345-1-4

PUNTILLERO PRESS
La Crescent • Minnesota

For Barbara, with love.

Table of Contents

Lleyellyn: from the Welsh meaning
"Lion like," leader, ruler.

Trempealeau Mountain:
"La montagne qui tremp a l'eau."
(The mountain whose foot is bathed in water.)

June 4

He was asleep. Dreaming. The exploding head jarred him awake. It sounded like a watermelon being crushed, but louder. Louder in his dream than it had been when it happened.

His racing pulse gradually slowed as his thoughts started to clear.

In his mind's eye he remembered the eviscerated body and the stench. The sound hadn't registered at first. It wasn't a melon he'd heard in his dream. He knew that immediately. It was a head. Mal's head.

When the train ran over the body, it mangled it beyond recognition. The carcass was in two main parts, split down the middle, a part on each side of the track tenuously connected by strands of a nylon jacket. The head had been obliterated.

In his dream the body was just as he remembered it. He was relieved that Mal was dead. Glad, actually. *The son-of-a-bitch had it coming.*

But there was something lurking in the back of his mind. It wasn't the sound or the memory of the body on the track. It was something else. At first he couldn't put a finger on it. Had he screwed up somewhere? Had they?

He was disoriented, forgetting for a few moments where he was, before getting his bearings and realizing he was back in the bunkhouse.

Montoya was snoring softly in the foreman's room. Sleeping soundly. Peacefully.

How would anyone be able to prove they both had left the ranch and tracked Mal down? No one could. He was sure of it.

They hadn't traveled together. Montoya had planned carefully. Everything had gone smoothly. They were home free.

Montoya had driven east in a borrowed rental car while he hitched rides and avoided public transportation altogether. They paid cash for everything. There was no paper trail. No one had recognized them in Winona or anywhere else after they left Montana. No one back there knew Montoya.

Montoya wasn't scheduled to see his parole agent until next week. Irene had been away in Denver for some conference.

No one could have known they had gone after Mal, the fugitive.

And yet there was something in the back of his mind he couldn't quite put his finger on. Everything had gone according to plan. He was sure of it.

He started to doze off again.

Then it came to him. *Shit! I mailed that damn check to Tole at that truck stop back in Wisconsin.*

Several days earlier...

CHAPTER ONE

May 13

He lay with his eyes closed, listening to see if anyone was moving about in the house. He didn't hear anyone. The TV was quiet. A block away a dog was barking, and he heard the far-off sound of a train whistle. The place was empty.

He had the best night sleep he'd had in a week. Mal hadn't come home. When Mal was around he was usually drunk. Sometimes high. Or both. Usually swore at his mother. Called him shit for brains, dip shit, or such when he wasn't punching him or throwing things.

His mother stepped between Mal and him, but she was risking injury to herself.

Mal's absence was a blessing.

He'd completed the Alternative School requirements before the end of the term. He was going to miss the formal graduation ceremony at the high school, but he'd picked up his diploma yesterday at the school office.

His head ached. His mouth was dry and he was thirsty. The stud in his tongue was slimy and it was sore from an infection.

Rolling over on the bare mattress, Lleyellyn Shay looked at the clock. The big hand was just past the eleven. The glass face on the clock was missing; so was the little hand. Sunlight poured through the un-curtained, grimy window. When he opened his eyes he saw the new tattoo on his forearm. *Kathy* it said. Instead of impressing his supposed girlfriend, she had gotten really pissed-off and stopped seeing him. He didn't know she spelled her name with a C.

He was relieved no one was around.

He stood up, stretched, then opened the two bolts and the padlock on his bedroom door and went in the bathroom. It was a wreck. Both light bulbs were burned out. Very little light shone through the mold on the pebbled window. The mirror was cracked and there were several rips in the shower curtain. Someone, probably his mother, had taped a note to the toilet seat. *Warning! Seat cracked!!!*

"Damn!" he said aloud. *Nothing ever works around here*, he thought, as he squeezed some toothpaste on his finger and brushed his teeth.

After putting on his pair of soiled denims and his beat-up Nikes, he went out to the kitchen. The sink was full of dirty dishes. The table was covered with empty cartons and drink cans. The only thing in the refrigerator was an almost-empty plastic milk jug. The top was missing. The milk had soured and had a greenish-yellow tinge. There was nothing in the house to eat. *Figures*, he thought. Mal, his stepfather, never brought home anything but beer and fast food.

Lleyellyn opened one of the pizza cartons on the table. Inside were several uneaten crusts. Mal usually hogged the whole pizza, but he hated crusts. He ate two or three pieces of crust, then rinsed out a glass and took a drink of water. He tested several pop cans on the counter and found one that was partly full. He tilted it toward the light to see if there were any cigarette butts inside, then took a drink. It tasted flat. Mountain Dew. He drained the can and gagged when he nearly swallowed something hard. Spitting it out, he saw nail clippings. *Mal, you asshole!*

Breakfast finished, he grabbed a balled-up tee shirt from

the floor next to his mattress and looked it over. It was stained and had several small holes under the arms and around neck. He put it on. It said *AC-DC World Tour* on the front.

Outside, the unmown grass was about a foot high. The bike he had ridden home was almost lost in the tall grass. He stood it up only to find that the rear tire was flat. "Nothing in this goddamned place ever works," he said to himself.

He was broke. Not a new experience. He had been fired from Culver's when he was late for work twice in one week. Mal never helped him out. His mother would try, but she was afraid of her husband. He just had to get out of there somehow.

As he started down the street toward downtown, he realized that it was Wednesday, trash pickup day. Bags of sorted trash were set out for Waste Management to pick up. They usually came mid-afternoon. Usually the recycling truck came by later.

A grocery cart had rolled to the edge of the parking lot at Econo Foods. He took the cart, and pushed it a block and a half to the first alley he came to. As he proceeded down the alley, he placed every bag of aluminum cans he could see in the cart. He tied some of the bags to the handle and others to the sides. There was no one around as he scoured the alleys and picked up bagged cans. He was pretty sure no one cared if he took the cans, but he didn't want to get in an argument about it with anyone.

At one house, midway down the block, someone had hung washing on the line to dry. He looked around carefully. Nobody was around. The garage was empty. He grabbed an *I Love London* tee shirt from the line and quickly replaced it with his own.

In less than an hour his shopping cart was as full as he could get it. It looked unwieldy as he pushed it along, but even fully loaded it was lighter than it appeared.

It was a short walk to the recycling center near the railroad tracks. He pushed the cart into the yard at Alten Scrap Metals and stopped at the scales. The old guy who handled the aluminum was in his little shack.

"Back again, I see," he said. "You know the drill."

Shay dumped the cans into a big plastic barrel. The attendant weighed the cans and wrote down the total. He filled the barrel five or six times.

"Well, let's see, you got sixty-eight point three pounds. Take this slip in the office. They'll pay you."

As he started off, the old guy said, "And don't forget to take the shopping cart with you when you leave."

He entered the office. The clerk was busy talking to some truck drivers. He waited his turn and looked at several posters and some of the notices on the bulletin board on the wall. He paid particular attention to a sign that said *Today's Prices. Aluminum 37 cents a pound. Copper $3.035.* A poster tacked up by the Burlington Northern Santa Fe Railroad wanted bids to remove old telegraph lines, poles, wire, insulators - the whole lot.

Before the conversation at the counter had gone on too long, the clerk looked over at Lleyellyn and said, "Hi there, London, what can I do for you?"

He was slow to catch on, before realizing the clerk was referring to his new tee shirt. Without comment he handed the slip to the clerk.

"Sixty-eight point three pounds of aluminum at thirty seven cents per pound," he said, punching a calculator. "That's twenty-five forty one. You want cash?"

"Yes, Sir. Thanks," Lleyellyn said.

The clerk handed him a twenty, five ones and some change.

"Don't spend it all in one place."

He got to McDonald's about two. A girl his own age with Becky on her name tag stood behind the counter waiting for his order.

"Two quarter-pounders from the dollar menu," he said.

She took his order. He paid $2.13. As the clerk made change, she said, "Nice shirt. My brother has one just like it. Have you been to London?"

Taken aback that the victim of his tee shirt thievery had spotted the stolen shirt so soon, he glanced at her briefly, then looking down, mumbled, "No. I got this shirt from a friend."

Lleyellyn found a table where someone had left their tray, wrappers and an empty plastic soft drink cup containing ice and an inch of dark colored soda. He picked up the tray and placed it in the trash receptacle – except for the cup. He dumped out the ice, briefly rinsed it with a squirt of cola and then filled it with fresh ice and Mountain Dew.

He was ready to point out the Free Refills sign if anyone said anything. He sat at the table and enjoyed lunch. He glanced over once or twice at the girl who had waited on him. She was busy waiting on customers and didn't appear to be thinking about the stolen shirt he was wearing.

His visit to the scrap metal dealer had given him an idea.

After he finished lunch, he walked directly to Ace Hardware where he bought a roll of duct tape.

He returned home. There was still no one there. He used the duct tape to repair the broken toilet seat. While he was at it, he taped up the cracked mirror and also taped over the rips in the shower curtain, but that didn't work too well. The tape wouldn't adhere to the soap scummed vinyl. He thought his mother might appreciate that he had at least tried to repair something.

Lleyellyn rummaged around in the garage until he found the fencing tool he was looking for. It was the pair his grandfather had used to mend barbed-wire fence on the farm.

Shay put the tool in his back pocket, grabbed a pair of flannel work gloves from the work bench in the garage, and the roll of duct tape. He walked toward the river until he came to the railroad tracks.

He walked along the tracks until he was out of the view of any buildings and out of sight of anyone at the railroad crossing. The telegraph lines the railroad wanted removed paralleled the tracks for as far as he could see. Some of the poles tilted. Many of the glass insulators were broken or missing. Some of the strands of wire were sagging and a few were down.

He looked around cautiously to make doubly sure no one was around. There were metal spikes hammered into the poles for steps. He climbed a telegraph pole, reached out along the cross piece as far as he could, and used his grandfather's fencing tool to cut all of the wires leading to and from the pole so that eight strands of wire fell away on each side. He did the same at the next pole in each direction. When he finished there were a total of eight strands of copper wire lying between each set of poles, sixteen strands in all.

Shay carefully rolled up each length of wire into a coil which he wrapped with enough duct tape so it wouldn't spring loose and uncoil. He counted sixteen coils when he was finished.

The whole effort had taken less than an hour. He put all sixteen coils in the weeds on the bank next to the track. The coils were a lot heavier than he expected. He wasn't sure, but he thought each coil must weigh close to forty-five, maybe fifty pounds.

Lleyellyn tried to carry two coils at a time, one in each hand, but that didn't work. Too damn heavy. So he picked up each coil, one at a time, and carried each one back along the tracks about a quarter mile until he reached the crossing. He stacked the coils near the railroad crossing sign making sure they were hidden in the weeds and tall grass. Two times freight trains came by. He stood off to the side each time. He waved at one of the engineers who returned the wave. He didn't see anyone in the engine of the second train. Both were heading toward the Twin Cities.

It took him the better part of three hours to carry all of the coils to the crossing. It was nearly five o'clock when he was done. He realized that the scrap yard would be closing soon.

He made sure all of the coils were well hidden in tall grass before he walked home. As he approached the house, he saw Mal's pickup was not parked in the yard. His mother was in the kitchen putting a kettle on the stove when he walked in.

"Hi!" she said. "Want some mac and cheese?"

"Sure, Ma. Where's Mal?"

"Who knows. Your guess is as good as mine," she said. "And, hey, thanks for fixing the toilet seat and stuff."

Dinner wasn't elegant, but at least it was dinner and he enjoyed being alone with his mother. There was nothing like a home-cooked meal. They didn't talk much, but several times his mother glanced at him, on the verge of saying something. Finally, after he had helped himself to seconds, she put down her fork, took a sip of coffee and looked at him.

"I know how Mal's been treating you. I think you've got to find a way to get out of here. Get on your own. Away from here. Away from Winona. I worry what he'll do next."

"What about how he treats you?"

"So far I've been able to handle Mal by myself. But I am worried about you. Especially when he's been drinking."

He was afraid of Mal himself. Mal was drunk every night. He was a mean drunk.

"I've got a few bucks I can give you so you can go somewhere."

He looked at her, not sure how much he should tell her.

"Ma, I don't need your money. I've got a job lined up. I should get paid soon. I've been planning to leave."

His mother didn't say anything at first. Then she took his right hand in hers, a serious expression on her face.

"Son, I know it's been hell for you. With your schooling

done, Mal will be even worse. He resents having you around. He doesn't bring in much money for us, but he claims he does, and he says he uses his money to cover your room and board. He's unreasonable. I don't want you to go, but I'd rather have you somewhere safe. Once you're gone, I plan to get out, too. Maybe move in with your grandmother for a while."

"As soon as I get paid, I plan to leave right away. Maybe in the next day or two. When I do, I'll contact you. Let you know I'm okay and where I am," he said.

"That's good, hon. But don't write me here. You better write to me at Gramma's. I don't want Mal to know where you are. And better not call me either. If Mal finds out he'll go off on a rant. I don't want him going through the phone bills trying to figure out where you're calling from."

CHAPTER TWO

May 14

Lleyellyn got up early the next morning. His mother had already gone to work. Mal was snoring loudly in the living room. For once he hadn't heard him come home. When he looked out Mal's pickup was parked a few feet from the front door.

Shay got dressed, then went down to McDonald's and ordered a Value Meal breakfast and a couple milks. When he was finished, he called Central Taxi and ordered a cab. The cab arrived three minutes later. He directed the driver to the rail-road crossing where he had hidden the wire.

"Stop here," he said. "Open the trunk. I need to load some stuff."

The driver stayed in the car as he loaded the coils of wire. It didn't take long. The taxi was an older Chevy Caprice with a huge trunk. The coils of wire took up most of the room and the rear of the taxi sagged under the load. Finally, he slammed the lid, got back in the vehicle, and said, "Take me to Alten Scrap Metal. Hauser Street. Know the place?"

"You bet. You know, it's a good thing I put heavy duty springs on this baby," the driver said. "I'm going to just go slow and avoid bumps the best I can to be safe."

When they got to the scrap yard, Lleyellyn got out. He was greeted by the same old guy who had weighed the aluminum cans the day before.

"What you got for me today, son?"

"I've got a bunch of copper wire. What's the copper price today?"

"You'll have to ask in the office. I just weigh it."

Lleyellyn Shay carried the coils from the cab to the scale. The employee precisely weighed the stack of coiled wire as a single unit and handed him the weigh slip.

"Looks like five hundred eighty-eight point six pounds," he said, reading the slip as he handed it to Shay.

As he had the day before, he headed to the office. Before he got there, the cab driver called out, "You want me to wait, or what?"

"Yeah, wait. I need to get back down town when I'm done here."

"The meter's running."

Inside, he presented the slip to a girl behind the counter.

"Hi!" she said, looking at the slip, "Copper. Today's buy price is three dollars point oh two two four." Then tapping the numbers on her calculator, she added, "That's one thousand seven hundred seventy-eight dollars and ninety eight cents. Okay?"

"Sure. I'll take cash."

"Anything over a hundred dollars is by check. We don't keep that much cash on hand," she said.

She printed out the check and handed it to him.

"Looks like a good day."

"Yes. Sure is, thanks."

He asked the cab driver to take him to the Town and Country Bank. He had noticed the check was drawn on the Alten account there. As the cabby waited, Lleyellyn went inside, showed the teller his state identity card, and cashed the check.

"How do you want it?" the teller asked.

He looked at her not sure just what she was driving at.

"Would hundreds, fifties and twenties be okay?" she finally asked.

"Oh, yeah. Sure. Thanks."

After the teller carefully counted out the money, Lleyellyn rolled up the stack of bills and stuffed them in his right front pocket and put the change in the left.

"Thanks, again," he said.

Returning to the cab, he told the driver to take him to the Amtrak station.

"How much?" he asked when they got there. The meter read one hundred nineteen dollars and twenty cents.

"One nineteen twenty plus the freight charge. That's one hundred twenty-nine dollars and twenty cents. Make it one twenty-nine even."

"Here, keep this," Shay said, handing the driver a hundred dollar bill and a fifty. "Thanks."

He talked to the Amtrak agent. An east bound train was due in at about ten AM, but it was running a half hour late. The west bound train wasn't expected until eight that evening. He bought a one-way ticket to Portland, Oregon.

He spent the afternoon buying clothes and a small suitcase. Then on a whim, he went to Lenny's Barbershop and got both a haircut and a shave. Finally he stopped back at McDonald's and treated himself to a Big Mac and a chocolate shake. Before leaving, he went to the men's room, changed into new clothes: briefs, Levi's and a flowered Hawaiian shirt. He carefully hung the I Love London tee shirt on a bar over the door to one of the stalls. His old pants, which were filthy and worn, he threw in the trash. He hoped that Becky would somehow get her brother's tee shirt back to him.

oOo

The depot was deserted. A sign near the ticket window read: *Ticket Agent Will be on Duty One Hour Before Scheduled Departure.*

The west bound Empire Builder was due in at 7:50 PM. The clock on the wall read six forty-seven.

Lleyellyn went outside and placed his small valise on a metal bench on the platform. It was a comfortable spring evening. There was no one waiting. A few hundred yards to the west a freight engine sat idling; two crew members standing off to the side occasionally talking on their hand-held transceivers.

He had never ridden Amtrak before. Years ago, his grandparents had taken him on a short train ride on a vintage train with a steam locomotive near Baraboo, Wisconsin. That had been when he was about five or six, he thought.

Just before seven, a uniformed railroad attendant walked onto the platform from the direction of the parking lot.

"Good evening. Waiting for the train?"

"Yes, Sir. Is it running on time?" Shay asked.

"I'm not sure. Come inside. We'll go check."

He followed the agent inside. The agent went through a door marked *Private* and reappeared almost immediately behind the barred ticket window.

"Well, let's see. It says the train left Tomah, Wisconsin right on schedule. Due into La Crosse about seven-twenty. On time. So far. I expect it in here right on schedule. About ten to eight. Need a ticket?"

"No. Thanks. I have one."

He went outside and sat on the bench. The idling freight train had started to move, creeping east at a very slow speed.

After waiting alone for about half an hour, a family of four pulling two large rolling suitcases walked onto the platform from the direction of the parking lot and sat at one of the other benches. Shay overheard enough of their conversation to know that they were on their way to Minneapolis.

Several more people showed up a few minutes later. A young black man wearing a throwback Lakers jersey with the name *JABBAR* on the back took a seat next to Lleyellyn.

"Train on time?"

"The agent said yeah. Due at ten to eight," Lleyellyn said.

"That'll be a first. Where're you goin'?"

Lleyellyn hesitated for a few seconds.

"I'm heading west. Portland," he said, paused, and added, "Oregon."

A train whistle sounded from the east.

"Here it comes!" the youngest of the Minneapolis-bound family shouted.

A blue-trimmed silver-colored engine was approaching. As it got closer and slowed it looked a lot bigger than he had expected. The locomotive, two baggage cars and several passenger cars passed by before the train came to a complete stop. He was surprised to see twenty-five or thirty people on the platform. They had showed up at the last minute. Most carried luggage. The doors of at least three of the passenger cars opened and uniformed attendants hopped down and placed matching yellow steps on the walkway before anyone was allowed to get off the train.

"Folks, line up here if you're getting on the train. Have your tickets ready. I'll tell you what car to get on when everyone has detrained," a woman in a blue uniform shouted.

It didn't take long for the disembarking passengers to get out of the way. He heard the conductor say, "Okay. Minneapolis, third car down. The attendant will tell you where to sit."

Most of the passengers seemed to be going to Minneapolis. A middle-aged woman in line in front of him was going to Red Wing.

"This car here, Ma'am. Get on here for Red Wing, Minnesota."

Lleyellyn Shay held out his ticket. The conductor looked at it.

"All the way to the end of the line," she said. "The Portland car is up front. See that step about three cars up toward the engine? That's where you go. Someone will help you find your seat."

He carried his bag up to the indicated car and stepped aboard. No one else had been headed to the Portland car.

"Welcome aboard," a jovial, slender African-American attendant said. "Put your bag on this shelf. We'll go up the steps. Pretty crowded today, but there's an open seat. Follow me."

He stowed his bag and followed the attendant up the steps. He heard a train whistle and felt the train start to move.

The attendant led him toward the front of the car.

"Here's the last vacant seat. The other seats are taken. If there's no one there now they are either in the Dining Car or the Observation Car."

The aisle seat was empty. The attendant put up a card over the seat that said "1/PTL" and motioned Lleyellyn to the seat.

"The Dining Car is one car ahead. Meal reservations are closed for tonight. I'll be by for breakfast reservations later on. The Observation Car is three cars back. It's open until eleven. There's a snack bar there if you're interested. My name is Marcus. Let me know if you need anything."

"Okay. Thanks."

"Any questions?"

"No. I'm good."

Before Shay sat down, he saw that the window seat was fully occupied. A large ten-gallon hat hid the face of a skinny cowboy-looking guy slouched next to the window, apparently asleep. He had his feet propped up on a dark brown saddle.

Lleyellyn looked out the window. The train was picking up speed. He had never seen Winona from a train before. As the train crossed a busy intersection he was surprised to see cars backed up for several blocks. The train must have been stopped longer than he realized.

As he got more accustomed to his surroundings, Lleyellyn felt more comfortable. He adjusted the foot rest and reclined the seat back.

He was able to study his seat companion. The big hat hid the guy's face completely, but his hands, which were folded on his lap, looked like they belonged to a young person. He had propped a pair of polished, cordovan, high-heeled cowboy boots on the saddle, which matched the color of the boots. *Elk, maybe buffalo*, he thought. The cowboy was wearing tight blue jeans and a satiny black, western-cut shirt accented by a wide belt with a large engraved, silver buckle.

As they left the outskirts of town, the intercom came on.

"Last call for dinner. Reservations ready for Lowell. Jenson. Watts. Bustamonte and Winters."

As soon as the announcement ended, the cowboy pushed back his hat and started to get up.

"Excuse me, pardner. I just got called to dinner."

With that he stepped around Lleyellyn and headed toward the dining car.

Lleyellyn was settling into his seat when he noticed a dark brown wallet lying on the floor in front of his seat. It was the same color as the saddle. He realized immediately that the cowboy had dropped it.

He looked around. No one was paying any attention to him. Most of the passengers were watching the scenery roll by or reading.

He glanced toward the front of the train. The aisle was empty. He reached down and picked up the wallet. Carefully he opened it. There was a thick sheaf of bills inside. *Holy shit!* he thought to himself. *That cowboy's going to miss this as soon as he has to pay for supper.*

Shay turned toward the window holding the wallet close to his chest so no one could see it. He riffled through the thick sheaf of bills. There were twenty hundred dollar bills and some fifties and smaller bills.

At least twenty five hundred bucks, he said to himself. *Enough to set me up pretty good.*

He wasn't sure what to do. He was setting out to make a fresh start. *I can't start out stealing some guy's money*, he thought. Then, without second guessing himself, he stood up and headed for the dining car.

He was surprised by how bumpy the train was as he opened the doors between cars.

When he got to the dining car he looked through the window at the two rows of tables neatly covered with white tablecloths. He opened the door and entered. At first he didn't see the cowboy. Then he spied him about half way down on the right. He was reading the menu. His big hat was sitting next to him on the table.

Shay walked toward the cowboy's table. As he approached, the cowboy looked up. He was surprised to see how young he was – about his own age.

"Sorry to bother you," he said, "but, I think you dropped this."

He handed the billfold to the cowboy who looked at it and then up at him.

"Yes. It is mine," he said. Then he smiled. "'Preciate it. If I'd a lost this I'd be truly fucked. Thanks, buddy. Thanks a whole lot."

"No problem."

As Lleyellen turned to go, the cowboy said, "Wait! Have a seat. I'm just about to order. Let me get you something. It's the least I can do. Sorta, as a reward."

He paused a few seconds. Then he sat down across the table from the cowboy.

"You don't owe me nothin'. I can buy my own food. But I could eat something."

"No. No, I insist. Without that wallet I'd be in deep sheep-dip."

The waiter showed up then and the cowboy said, "I'll take the steak. Rare. Salad with the house dressing. And a Coke. My buddy here is going to order, too. One bill. For me."

Shay didn't hesitate.

"I'll have the same. But ranch dressing. And a Mountain Dew."

As the waiter left, the cowboy said, "I'm Tole Winters," and held out his hand.

They shook hands, and he said, "Lleyellyn Shay. Glad to meet you. Call me Lou Ellen. Lot of people do."

They each smiled expectantly.

Finally Shay said, "With your outfit and saddle and all I can see you're some kind of cowboy. Where you going?"

"Heading to Miles City, Montana and then on to Bend, Oregon. There's some pretty big rodeos coming up. Saddle broncs for me. My first pro rodeo."

"No kidding. How long you been doing the rodeo thing?"

"Not very. I graduated a semester early, but was still eligible to compete at the NHSR. The National High School Rodeo. In Tomah. Tomah, Wisconsin. Close to home. Lucky enough to win the saddle bronc event last month. My uncle thought I was pretty good. He's given me money for my entry fees. Bought me the train ticket. Advanced me the money there in my wallet. I'm going to try and earn a little prize money."

"Sounds like dangerous work," Shay said. "Prize money any good?"

"Well, not sure. Guess it depends on how many entries

there are. It costs a seventy-five dollar entry fee. Part of the total of all the entry fees goes to the winner. Lesser amounts to two through five. If you don't place you get nada," Tole explained.

"How many will be competing?"

"Not sure of that, either. If it's a big event, maybe thirty entries. Maybe more. I guess maybe two, three thousand for the winner."

"Is it worth it? I mean, you could get hurt, right?"

"Well, it's maybe a couple thousand for three eight second rides. Works out pretty good on a per hour basis - if you win," Winters said with a grin. "But, and it's a big but, only if you hang on long enough."

"You mean if you don't place in the top five you get nothin'?"

"Well, the way it works, some guys have sponsors. Wrangler, maybe Levi's. Copenhagen tobacco. Stetson hats. Justin boots. Even Viagra. And some others. Those guys get paid just for showing up and wearing the sponsor's logos. I'm just trying to get started. I'll have to make a good showing before I can join the PRA and hope to attract a sponsor. All my high school championship did is get my toe in the door."

"Geez. Good luck. Hope you win some big bucks."

The waiter served their steaks which looked and smelled delicious. Lleyellyn couldn't recall the last time he'd sat down to eat at a restaurant other than McDonald's. He watched Tole, and following his example unfolded the big, white cloth napkin and placed it on his lap.

They both cut off a piece of steak and took a mouthful.

"Not too bad," Lleyellyn said.

After taking a confirmatory taste, Tole looked up at him and said, "You know you're right, this is mighty fine material. I'm hungrier than I thought."

After they had eaten in silence for a while, Tole set his

knife and fork down, then used his napkin.

"How about you, Lou. Lou Ellen? Where you headed?"

Deciding there was no reason to hide anything, Shay said, "I'm going to Portland, Oregon to look for a job. Trying to make a fresh start. Hell, I'm trying to start over as far away from my stepfather as I can get. I've got a few bucks I hope will last 'til I find a job of some kind."

"How old are you?"

"Eighteen. You?"

"Same."

They each digested this information and their steaks for a few moments before Winters said, "I should get into Glasgow, Montana about noon tomorrow. Then I'll check in at a motel. The rodeo is next weekend, so I've got plenty of time to catch a ride or maybe take a bus down to Miles City. The one in Bend, Oregon is a week later."

"Well, I'm supposed to get into Portland on Monday morning," Shay said.

oOo

When they returned to their seats, Tole said, "I've gottta get some sleep. I was awake all night. Going-away party. Some friends threw it. Can't keep my eyes open much longer."

He placed his seat back as far as it would go, stretched his feet out on his saddle, and pulled his hat down over his face. He fell asleep almost immediately.

Shay was wide awake. He sat there watching the Mississippi river. It wasn't fully dark yet, and the lighting appeared to make even the slightest detail stand out sharply. He thought about Tole. *What an unusual name. Tole. How can I talk? Lleyellen is weirder. Lou Ellen.*

Is Tole a nickname, too? Tole was pretty lucky to get a big send-off from his friends. His uncle gave him some money to get started, and he has a goal. That was important. He had a chance to hit it big competing in rodeos. What a contrast from my own situation. We're about the same age. No one saw me off. No one gave me any money. I left to get away from home; especially that no good jerk, Mal. The only money I have is what I got from the copper wire I salvaged.

He watched a tow boat pushing twelve barges heading upstream.

Well, at least I'm going somewhere, he thought. *I can make a fresh start, get a job, start over. Things will work out.*

He slid his tongue over the stud. The damn thing was a nuisance. It always felt strange. The infection never seemed to clear up. People looked at him funny when he talked. He should never have had it done. Stupid tongue piercing. Why'd he do it? Lleyellyn reached into his mouth and unscrewed the stud and took it out. He decided his new start wouldn't include piercings. He put it in his pants pocket and settled back. He ran his tongue against the roof of his mouth. *Feels better already,* he thought, before dozing off.

oOo

Shay vaguely heard someone say, "Red Wing. Red Wing, Minnesota," but didn't fully wake up. Later the announcement, "Minneapolis – St. Paul. Next stop Minneapolis – St. Paul. If you are detraining here, please look around, above and under your seat. Don't forget your luggage. We'll be stopping in the Twin Cities, Minneapolis and St. Paul in about eight minutes."

Now everyone was awake. No one in his car was getting off, but some people were standing and stretching. Marcus, the attendant, came through the car.

"Folks, if you want to smoke, this is the place. We'll be

here for fifteen minutes. If you get off don't stray too far."

Tole pushed his hat back and stretched.

"Boy, I feel a whole lot better," he said. "What time you got?"

"Almost eleven. I fell asleep, too."

Everyone in the car settled down pretty quickly. No one got off for a smoke.

When the train pulled out of the station it was obvious that the Midway Station was nowhere near downtown Minneapolis or St. Paul.

"Hey!" Tole said. "I've got some Pepsis in my bag. Want one?"

As they opened their drinks, Lleyellyn said, "I was thinking. The difference between you and me is that you're heading somewhere to do something you want to do. Me, I'm running away from something I need to get away from."

Winters thought about this for a while, took a drink of Pepsi, and said, "I'm not too sure about that. I think my uncle gave me the money and paid the entry fees to get me out of the house. I know he's hoping I'll get by on my own from now on. And, I hope so, too."

"How come your uncle?"

"After my dad died, my aunt and uncle took me in. My mother just fell apart when dad died. She's been in a facility ever since. Then my aunt died about a year ago. My uncle's okay, but he's raised all his own kids and then me, and he wants to take it easy. I don't plan on going back."

"Well," Shay said. "At least you've got the rodeo thing."

Tole looked over at him and smiled.

"I'll let you in on a little secret. I was real lucky to win the event at the Nationals. I only started riding a year or so ago. Had pretty good arm strength working out on the wrestling team. A friend was competing in a rodeo and I went along for the hell of it. I tried it and did okay. I rode about fifteen or twenty times during the year and stayed on about half the time. At the Nationals I was real lucky. By the luck of the draw, the best riders got bucked off by the best horses. My first ride was an easy one. I got a low score, but some got nothing. I was the only rider to stay on in both rounds. Another lucky break. But I wasn't the best, just the luckiest. And here I am. I know I'm not the best saddle bronc rider around, not by a long shot."

Lleyellyn mulled this over.

"Aren't you kinda afraid of entering a professional rodeo?"

"Sure," Tole said. "But I'm going to give her a try. It's now or never."

"I was wondering. You know, curious. What kind of name is Tole anyway? Nickname?"

"Everybody calls me Tole. I tell everybody that's my name. But it says Tolland Merriweather Winters on my birth certificate." He turned and looked directly at Lou Ellen. "You know I don't think I've ever told anybody that."

"Wow! Okay. Tole it is," he said. "Great cowboy name."

CHAPTER THREE

May 15

The train continued west through the night. Lleyellyn slept through an early morning stop at Fargo, North Dakota.

About six, an announcement was made from the dining car.

"I'll be through to take dining car reservations for breakfast. First serving at seven. Seven A.M. Central Daytlight Savings time."

They signed up for the seven o'clock seating.

"I'm hungry," Lleyellyn said. "And I'm buying. My turn."

The dining car was nearly full by the time they took their places at the same table where they had been seated the night before.

This time Lleyellyn ordered the country breakfast: eggs, ham, hash browns and toast with a Mountain Dew. Tole opted for a waffle, bacon and orange juice.

"I told you about me," Tole began. "Why are you going to Portland, Oregon?"

He told Tole about his plans to start over in Portland. How he wanted to make a clean break from the bad situation he had with Mal and about how he had raised the money for his trip. Tole listened but didn't say much. He was a good listener.

After breakfast, they returned to their seats.

oOo

The Security Supervisor for the Burlington Northern Santa Fe Railroad patrolled the tracks between Minneapolis and La Crosse at least once a week. He noticed the missing telegraph wire just a day after someone had cut down the wire. There had been copper wire thefts occurring more and more frequently with the steady rise in the price of copper.

The railroad's telegraph wire was a unique gauge not used for any other purpose. It didn't take the supervisor long to track down the missing wire and identify the thief as soon as he stopped by Alten Scrap and talked to the clerk behind the counter.

"Why, yes. Just yesterday. A guy, nineteen or so, brought in nearly four hundred pounds of that kind of wire," the clerk said, impressed by the railroad line supervisor's identification and trying to be helpful. "Yes, it's right here on the screen. Five hundred eighty-eight point six pounds, in fact. Paid him by check. One thousand seven hundred seventy-eight dollars and change."

"Who sold the wire to you?" the railroad man asked.

"L-L-E-Y-E-L-L-Y-N, I'm not sure how you pronounce it. Lleyellyn Shay. He lives here in town. Past customer. Mostly aluminum until yesterday."

"Address?"

The clerk read the address from the screen, then asked, "Is there a problem?"

oOo

The railroad's Security Supervisor prepared a formal Report of Theft and took it to the Sheriff's office.

"Here's my report on the stolen copper wire that I called

you about. Lleyellyn Shay's the thief. Value exceeds a thousand dollars. Felony amount. Criminal trespass, too. We want this case prosecuted," he said. "And restitution."

oOo

The Sheriff consulted with the County Attorney. The prosecutor prepared a Criminal Complaint alleging that one Lleyellyn Fellows Shay had committed felony theft and criminal trespass. Then he drafted an Arrest Warrant for the approval and signature of a Judge.

The County Attorney told the Sheriff, "Easy case for your office. You should get the railroad to do more of your work."

"Shit! Those bastards are only interested in your office getting results and their money. Restitution is what they are after," the Sheriff replied. "We're becoming their damned collection agency.

oOo

An Arrest Warrant must be signed by a Judge before it can be used to take someone into custody. As was customary, the County Attorney called the Judge's law clerk to see if he could set up a time to meet with the Judge in her chambers. Nearly every day there were Arrest Warrants, Search Warrants, and other papers that the Judge had to approve and sign.

Judge Jensen had been on the bench about eight years. Before that, she had served three terms as the County Attorney. Her husband was a retired deputy sheriff. Between the two of them, there wasn't much that went on in the county they didn't know about.

The County Attorney, Ken Watts, had succeeded Harriet Jensen when she was appointed to the bench. She was familiar with his duties. She didn't always agree with his way of doing business, but the two maintained a formal cordiality.

"Come in, Mr. Watts. What have you got for me?" the judge said by way of greeting.

"Not too much today, Judge, Search Warrant application. One request for an Arrest Warrant," he said, handing the documents to the Judge.

While the Judge reviewed the Search Warrant Application, Watts looked at the pictures on the walls of the Judge's chambers. There were pictures of past Judges and some of her family. Displayed prominently was a section under the stenciled words *Honor Roll* featuring photographs of past defendants in her court who had completed probation and become successful in one way or another. The Judge was a firm believer in rehabilitation and very proud of the members listed on her *Honor Roll*.

After signing the Search Warrant, the Judge turned to the County Attorney and said, "Tell me about this Arrest Warrant."

"Lleyellyn Fellows Shay. Maybe you know him. People call him Lou Ellen. Cut down copper telegraph wire along the BN right-of-way and called a cab to haul it to the scrap yard. The price of copper is at a record high. He got over a thousand dollars for his efforts. Half day's work, it seems. He took the Amtrak to Portland, Oregon, night before last. The railroad wants him prosecuted and full restitution. It's a strong case, your Honor."

The Judge looked over her wire-rimmed spectacles at Watts.

"You know, the railroad hasn't used those telegraph lines for at least fifteen years. Everything today is by cell phone, GPS, radio or computer. It's only now that they show concern. I agree, it looks like a crime." After a pause, she added, "This would have been a misdemeanor a few years back when copper was cheap."

The prosecutor looked at the judge, but didn't say anything.

She continued. "I know this kid. Heck, Lou Ellen played T-ball and Little League baseball with my son. His father was a great guy. After he was killed at the plant, things went to hell for his widow and her son. Then his mother hooked up with that Malverne Dotwich character. Malverne Lester Dotwich, if memory serves. Dotwich had a daughter. Sally, I think. Lleyellyn's stepsister. Left home a year or two ago. Dotwich has been in and out of jail and prison more times than I can remember."

"Well, Dotwich's been on my radar for some time, too," the County Attorney said.

"My point is this. Shay has no chance if he doesn't get out of here and away from his stepfather. The railroad is not your typical crime victim. I'm going to sign the warrant, but I'm going to add a little to it," the Judge said.

She wrote a line at the bottom of the Arrest Warrant and then she dated and signed it.

"Enforceable within this state only," she had added in bold, dark blue handwriting.

oOo

The attendant, Marcus, came through the car carrying a stack of newspapers.

"You boys want something to read?" he asked, as he handed a newspaper to Shay.

"I'm going to the washroom. Freshen up a little," Tole said.

Shay opened the paper. Wall Street Journal. He looked through it. No pictures. No sports. No comics. An article about the business dealings of super-star athletes caught his eye. He finished the article just as Tole returned.

"You ought to read this," Lleyellyn said. "Big time stars like Michael Jordan and Tiger Woods have a whole staff to handle stuff like autographs, answering letters. Even setting up web sites and supervising fan clubs."

Tole looked at him.

"You get famous, you'll have to get a staff, too."

"Fat chance. Rodeo ain't like golf or basketball. Those sports," Tole said.

"You know Kobe Bryant?" Lleyellyn said. "He has a guy that handles the groupies that follow him everywhere. Has them sign a release if they want to see Kobe in private."

"No kidding?" Tole said.

"As soon as you become a famous rodeo star you'll need a full time staff just like those guys. You'll need to have someone protect you from the groupies..." Lleyellyn said, before being interrupted.

"I kid you not. If I get famous, I'll handle the groupies on my own," Tole said, grinning. "I'm not thinking of fame, though, Bud. I'm just hoping to get my boot in the door."

oOo

By the time the train got to Wolf Point, Montana, they had told each other their life stories.

"I'm getting off at the next stop," Tole said. "Why don't you get off with me? You ain't really got any place you have to be."

"I'm going to Portland. Ticket's all paid for."

"I know. But you don't have any real reason to get to Portland right now. No schedule. No appointments or anything. Get off here. I'll get us a motel room. Stay with me. No charge. I bet you'd get hired right off at the rodeo grounds. You know. Selling tickets. Maybe unload feed. Something."

He thought about it. Tole was right. He had a ticket but really no place he had to be.

"What the hell," he said. "Okay. I'll do 'er."

oOo

When they arrived at Glasgow an hour later Tole grabbed his saddle. Shay carried their duffel bags down the stairs and off the train. It was almost noon. A half-dozen passengers were waiting to board.

"You cowpokes have a great day," Marcus said. "Thanks for riding Amtrak."

They found out from the Amtrak ticket agent that there was no bus service to Miles City.

"Take a look at that bulletin board over by the water fountain. Private vans are available day and night."

Tole checked the board, called a few numbers, and arranged for a van to pick them up at two.

"How about a cup of coffee or something?" Tole said.

"Let's get a couple of sandwiches. It's a long way to Miles City."

They bought lunch at a café on First Avenue and ordered drinks. Coffee for Tole. Mountain Dew for Lleyellyn.

"First thing I'm gonna do when I get to Miles City is go to the bank," Tole said. "I'm going to put most of my money in a checking account and get a cash card."

"What for?"

"Feel safer with less cash in my pocket. I've got all my money on me. More than a thousand dollars. It's all I've got. Can't afford to lose it. Again."

"You're probably right. Maybe I should too."

"How much you got on ya?" Tole asked.

"About the same as you. Maybe a little more."

oOo

Tole carried his saddle into the Wells Fargo Bank in Miles City and set it down in front of a teller's window. No one seemed to give them any special looks.

"Can I help you boys?" the teller asked.

"Yes, Ma'am," Tole said. "We'd each like to open up checking accounts and get cash cards."

"I can help you with that. Need to see some state-issued photo ID. Minimum deposit to open an account is five hundred dollars. That okay with you?"

They each produced their IDs. Tole, his Wisconsin driver's license; Lleyellyn, a Minnesota state identification card.

"Here for the rodeo?" the teller asked, making small talk as she completed opening the accounts.

"Yes, Ma'am," Tole said.

"He's a bronc rider," Shay said. "Saddle broncs."

CHAPTER FOUR

May 17

Tole tugged his hat down tight. He nodded to the guys manning the gate. He was ready. As ready as he could get.

"Ladies and gentlemen. Our next bronc rider is a young man from Wisconsin. Tole Winters. The National High School Saddle Bronc Champion. Give him a big hand. This is his first professional rodeo."

The voice of the announcer echoed from the loudspeakers as the gate flew open.

The horse, Durango Sparky, jumped sideways out of the chute. Tole leaned back in the saddle, his right hand held high, and spurred with both feet.

"Looks like they know what they're doing," the announcer said. "The cowboy. And the horse."

Durango Sparky was tall and rangy. A pinto with three white stockings. He had been ridden only twice in two years. A very good mount.

Tole had talked to some of the other cowboys. They had given him the book on Durango Sparky.

"Comes out sideways," one old boy from Mesquite, Texas, had told him. "Then he'll turn left and buck front and back, then turn again."

Tole was ready. But the horse didn't turn left. He bucked hard three straight times. Tole, who had started to lean for the expected left turn, lost his center of gravity for a second, but then got control and continued raking both sides of the horse with his spurs, his right hand held high. The crowd came to attention.

"Yessir, ladies and gentlemen, this high school champion is off to a good start," the announcer reported. "That's a mighty fine horse and this fella's giving him a darn good ride."

Tole couldn't hear the announcer. Every time the horse touched down Tole felt the jolt throughout his body. The pounding sounded like a bombardment in his head. The eight second clock was at four point two. Tole didn't know how much of the eight seconds was left.

Durango Sparky stopped bucking, feinted to the left and then turned right. Tole was leaning way over and started to fall. By sheer force of will he pulled himself upright as the horse started to run toward the fence.

Tole held on. The eight second horn sounded and the pickup riders moved in to assist. Just then Durango Sparky turned and bucked to the left and Tole lost his grip. He flew toward the fence and slammed into it. His right hand came down over the top rail. Lleyellyn winced in pain as his forearm hit the rail, and he crumpled to the ground.

"That was a great ride. Made the time. Looks like an eighty-six from the judges. Tole Winters is leading the competition."

Tole lay on the ground. His right forearm felt like it was broken. Several hands helped him up.

"Hell of a ride," one of them said. "Your arm okay?"

"Hurts. I think it's maybe broken," he managed through gritted teeth.

"Well pard, that's bronc riding," another competitor said. "Walk on over to the infirmary and get it checked out."

"Looks like that young feller got himself banged up a little on that top rail, folks. He'll get that looked after. He'll be back tomorrow for the next round rarin' to go," the announcer said.

Tole held his right wrist against his side with his left hand and headed for the infirmary. He was in pain. He felt like crying. No one seemed to think it was any big deal. He was aware that he had lasted the required eight seconds. He didn't hear his score. He didn't think he would be riding tomorrow night.

He saw an older mobile home under the grandstand. *RODEO INFIRMARY: Contestants and Staff Only* was hand-lettered on a sign next to the door.

Tole walked into the infirmary. Two other cowboys were sitting on plastic chairs in the waiting room. One was holding a bloody bandanna to his mouth; the other had his boot off. His foot was swollen and bent sideways.

"Accident?" the barefoot cowboy asked.

"Yeah. Damn horse bucked me off and I hit my arm on the top rail. Dusted, I think," Tole said. "You?"

"Unloading stock. Got stepped on by a damn horse. Ankle's probably broken. I'll be gimping around for a little while."

Tole turned to the other cowboy. He glanced back at Tole and removed the bandanna for a second so he could talk. His mouth was bloody.

"Lost a couple teeth when I got throwed. Hit something hard. Not even sure what."

A door opened and the doctor walked in. He was a short balding man with the butt of an unlit cigar protruding from his mouth.

"Okay. I'm going to have someone drive toothy here downtown to see a dentist. Ankle, I'm having the nurse get a bucket of ice to try and get the swelling down. You, arm fracture, come into the back room with me."

Tole was surprised to see that the clinic was well supplied.

"I'm Doctor Evans," he said as he introduced himself. "We're going to take an x-ray of that arm and then we'll put her in a cast."

The doctor and his assistant, a short middle-aged woman, were efficient. The x-ray revealed a simple fracture of the forearm with no displacement. He was given several pain pills and his arm was put in a cast that extended from his upper arm past his wrist and around his thumb.

"I hear you're leading the saddle bronc competition, young man. Been at this a long time?"

"No. No, Sir. I mean, this is my first professional rodeo," Tole replied.

"Well, they tell me you rode a tough, hard horse and rode him well. This little arm thing is a bit of bad luck. Some of the top riders didn't make the time tonight. I think you've got a good chance of winning," the doctor said.

"Winning? Hell, Doc, I don't think I can ride with a broken arm."

The doctor looked at Tole for a moment, then removed the cigar from his mouth.

"This is rodeo. Cowboys get busted up. Stove in. Mangled a bit. But most of 'em are tough as nails. They keep on going. You're lucky. You don't have to do nothing with that right arm tomorrow night except hold it up and hang on. You've got a doctor's permission to ride tomorrow night if you want to."

Tole looked at the doctor and was about to say something.

"Look, kid. It's up to you if you want to get back on tomorrow night. I've been working rodeos for more than twenty years. The life of a rodeo cowboy is not the easiest. Do what you want. But remember, you're leading the saddle bronc event. If you stay on tomorrow you'll have a good chance to cash a pretty big check no matter how you do. If you win, you'll do a whole lot better, get some great publicity, and maybe even a sponsor or two."

oOo

The beer tent was crowded. Blue-denim-clad men in wide-brimmed hats stood three-deep around the four-sided bar. Lleyellyn had been working at it since noon and the crowd had been steady.

He was glad for the job. Paid ten dollars an hour and he got some tips. Tole could take his chances riding bucking horses. He was certain he would be making at least two hundred dollars for the day.

"Hey, barkeep. Two more Coors over here," someone shouted and he hurried to fill two plastic cups.

There were half a dozen bartenders and they were all busy.

Shay knew that Tole's ride was probably over, but he hadn't had a chance to find out how he had done. It was too noisy to hear the grandstand announcer in the beer tent, and most of the drinking cowboys had stayed in the tent while the rodeo was going on.

"I'll take six over here. Buds," someone shouted and he filled the order.

At about ten-thirty the guy who had hired him sidled up to Lleyellyn and said, "You've been at it for a while now. Take a ten minute break. We'll manage."

Shay stooped under the counter and squeezed past the assembled beer drinkers. He walked over to the entrance to the arena. The grandstand was near standing room only. The crowd was going wild. The announcer was talking about the main event of the evening – bull-riding.

He walked over to the ticket booth. A lady inside was counting money. Ticket sales were finished for the night. Holding her place in a stack of twenty dollar bills with her finger, she looked up.

"Help you?"

"Yes, thanks. I was wondering how Tole Winters did in the saddle bronc event."

"Don't know. I just sell tickets and count the money." she said. "If I was you, I'd try the press tent. It's over next to the office. Behind the grandstand."

Lleyellyn followed the ticket lady's directions. There were only a few people around. Everybody was in the grandstand or at the beer tent. He saw a sign marked PRESS. The door was open and there was a paper-littered desk against the far wall. Two men inside appeared busy. He figured they were reporters. One was on the phone; the other was working at his laptop. Lleyellyn stood in the doorway until the guy on the phone looked up and motioned him inside and pointed to a chair. He waited until the phone call ended. The man at the laptop never stopped typing and never looked up.

"What can I do for you?"

"I wonder if you know how the saddle bronc event came out tonight. A friend of mine was in it."

"Let's see. Here's the Results Sheet. Only eight riders made the time. The leader with 86 points is a guy I never heard of. Tole Winters."

"Yeah, that's my friend."

"Well he's the lead story for the ten o'clock news. High school champion. First rodeo. Top score on a tough horse."

"Great!" Lou Ellen said. "Don't think he expected things to go that well."

"Listen. When you see him give this to him," the reporter said as he handed Lleyellyn his business card. "Ask him to give me a call about one tomorrow afternoon. I'd like to interview him for the radio station. Great personal interest story."

"Okay, sure will. Thanks for the info."

oOo

Business at the beer tent was brisk until closing time. When the crowd left, Shay helped stack the empty kegs and carried in some fresh ones for the next day. He emptied the trash barrels, then joined the other bartenders picking up empty cups and other litter. When they were done, they lined up single file at the far corner of the bar while the manager on the inside of the counter paid each one. Cash. No deductions. Nothing withheld. Ten dollars per hour. He was handed six twenty dollar bills.

"You'll be back tomorrow at noon?" the manager asked him after he had pocketed his pay.

"Yes sir. See you at twelve o'clock noon."

He walked away. With his tips he had a little over two hundred and fifty dollars in his pocket. He felt tired but elated as he started to walk back to the motel.

CHAPTER FIVE

May 18

The motel parking lot was full. Mostly pickups. The doors of nearly all the rooms were open. It was a warm night. Several parties were going on.

Room nine, where he and Tole were staying, appeared dark. The door was closed. It was about two.

Shay fumbled in his pants pocket for the key and opened the door. The TV was on, showing a black-and-white western. The sound was muted. No lights were on. In the pale bluish light he saw Tole spread-eagled on the bed.

He turned on the light and saw Tole with a big cast on his right arm.

"What the hell? I heard you're leading. What the fuck happened to your arm?"

Tole opened his eyes and focused them on Lleyellyn.

"It's broken. Hit my arm on the fence when I got throwed. Right after the horn sounded. Hurts like a goddamned hoot-owl."

"Man. Here I thought you were doing great. I talked to a radio station reporter. He said you got the top score."

Tole looked at his friend a minute, and then struggled to a sitting position.

"Let me tell you. These big league horses are a lot tougher than the ones I rode back home. Everything happened so fast I didn't know if I made the time or not. And then, shoot, look at my arm."

"Your cast must weigh a ton. How bad's it broken?"

"Well the doctor said there was no displacement. He even said I could ride itomorrow. Do the cowboy thing."

Shay thought this over.

"You don't have to ride, you know. Why screw up your arm, or something else?"

"I know there's some danger. I saw a guy in the doctor's office with a broken foot. Said a horse stepped on him. Another old boy was sitting there bleeding with a couple of teeth missing. He didn't even know how it happened. Hell, I hardly know how I busted my arm."

After a few minutes Lleyellyn stood up.

"Want anything? Water?"

"Yeah. A glass of water would be great. I need to take a pain pill the doc gave me."

Tole took the water and downed a pain pill. They sat there for a moment and then Shay said, "I'm going to wash up and get to bed. They want me back at work tomorrow at noon. You should get some sleep. You can think about riding tomorrow, or not, in the morning."

He turned out the light and crawled into the twin bed next to the window.

"See you in the morning, cowboy."

"Sleep tight," Tole said. Then added, "Say, how much did you make working the beer tent?"

There was no reply. Lleyellyn was asleep.

oOo

"Housekeeping!"

Shay heard something. There was a knock on the door.

"Housekeeping!"

"We're still in bed!" he shouted back.

He rolled over and looked at the clock. Ten thirty.

He could hear the shower in the bathroom and knew Tole was up. A ray of bright sunlight showed through a gap in the curtains.

Lleyellyn got out of bed as Tole came into the room, still drying his hair with a towel.

"See you're up. Working today?" Tole said.

"Not 'til noon," Lleyellyn replied. "How's your arm?"

"Aches a little. Not too bad. It's hard to use when you can't bend it."

Shay went into the bathroom, took a leak, and quickly showered. He took a pair of briefs from his backpack, put them on and added a tee shirt with *Real Rodeo* written across the front, then pulled on his jeans. He slipped four twenties in his right boot before putting it on.

"How about you? Going to try ridin' tonight?"

"Not sure. Event starts at seven. I'm still thinking on it," Tole said.

Shay suddenly remembered the reporter.

"Before I forget. A reporter gave me his card. Wants you to call him. Thinking of doing a story about you."

They both finished dressing and went across the street to the Big Sky Café.

"Tell me about your ride," Lou Ellen said, after they slid into a booth.

Tole looked at him for a moment.

"I was real nervous. Got there pretty early. Some of the old boys have been pros for years."

"How'd they treat you?"

"They didn't say much. A couple told me about the horse I drew. Durango Sparky. Others just wished me luck. Most of them were wearing protective braces or elbow padding and such. Seemed to be a superstitious bunch. Mostly pretty quiet."

"Anybody else at their first pro rodeo?" he asked.

"Not really. Not that I know of, anyway. One guy said he was back for the first time after healing up and there were two foreigners who were used to riding in another country. One from Australia. Other guy from South America. Argentina, I think," Tole said.

A waitress handed them a menu, but before glancing at it, Tole said, "I watched the first few riders from the top of the fence. Looked like what I was used to. Except the horses looked bigger and of course there was that big crowd."

Tole took a sip of water, and continued. "First guy up was a former points leader. He lasted about two seconds and came back swearing. I saw him fall. He didn't say anything about getting hurt. He just walked back through the chute, got in his pickup and drove off."

The waitress interrupted them and took their orders.

"What about the horse you drew?"

"Durango Shorty. Meant nothing to me. One of the guys told me he was a top points leader. Another guy had ridden him twice before. Or tried to. He told me some of his tendencies.

"When my number was called, I got on and everything seemed like other rodeos. Like the high school ones. The damned horse leaned against the stall and they had to push him over so I could get my legs in spurring position. I could see old Durango Sparky looking back at me the whole time. Seemed like he knew what he was doing.

"The ride seemed to last an hour, but I can't remember much. I spurred him as much as I could. I never heard the horn, and then he threw me toward the fence and I hit my arm on the top rung. I can't say I did a good job. I was lucky to last. Unlucky with my arm."

When the waitress brought their orders, Lleyellyn saw that Tole was having trouble cutting up his ham.

"Here, let me help you with that. I've got two good hands," he said as he cut the meat into bite-sized pieces. "Well, while you was putting in your time on the back of a horse, I was filling beer cups for a pretty thirsty bunch. Made ten bucks an hour. Plus tips. Two hundred and fifty bucks. A little more. Most I ever made in a day. Legit."

As they finished breakfast, the waitress filled Tole's cup and Shay emptied the last of a can of Mountain Dew into his glass.

"If you decide to try again tonight, I'd like to see it, but I'm supposed to work from noon to closing time. Maybe I'll ask for a break during your event. What time will that be?"

"They go in reverse order. I'm leading. I get to go last...if I decide to go at all," Tole said.

Tole looked at Lleyellyn who smiled back.

"Hey look. You don't have to ride if you don't want to. It's your neck. Your arm. Do what you want. I'm just glad I'm in the beer pouring business tonight, that's for sure."

As they were ready to leave. Shay glanced over and saw a newspaper sitting on the next table. It was the local sports page.

"Look at this!" he said and held it up for Tole to see. *WISCONSIN HIGH SCHOOLER LEADS BUCKING HORSE EVENT*, the headline read.

Tole reached for the paper. There was a photo under the headline. It was a picture of a cowboy on a bucking horse. They read the caption together. *Durango Shorty met his match last night. Tole Winters, the National High School Champion from Wisconsin, grabbed top saddle bronc honors in the first round with a high point total of 86. Winters will be trying to hold off several top riders tonight. Tickets available at the gate.*

Tole turned to his friend and grinned.

"Paper thinks I'm riding tonight," he said.

"Well, it's still your choice."

"Yeah, but I can't let my fans down."

"Fans? You mean me?"

Just then, the waitress came up behind them.

"Anything else for you boys?" she asked.

They both turned from the sports page to her. She was smiling back at them. About their age. Red-headed with freckles. She looked at the paper, then back at Tole.

"That's you! Ain't it?" she said. "You're that high school champion cowboy."

Neither of them replied at first. They looked at the waitress with her big name tag above her left breast. LaDonna Mae.

"Now, I know it's you," LaDonna Mae said. "Wait here."

They stood there looking sheepishly at each other, aware that several customers were watching them and studying the picture in the paper.

"Maybe you've got two fans," Tole said.

The waitress came back with a black felt marker.

"Sign the picture, would you? I'll put it up on the board."

"What shall I write?" Tole asked.

"Just say something. Put my name in it. LaDonna Mae. Capital L capital D," she said.

Tole took the marker and realized immediately that it was almost impossible to write with his arm in the cast.

"LaDonna Mae," he said. "I can't hardly write at all with this cast. Lleyellyn, my manager here, he signs these for me," he said glancing up at the waitress, then at Lleyellyn.

"Sign this for LaDonna Mae will you? That's LaDonna with a capital L capital D."

oOo

After they returned to the motel, Shay offered to help Tole carry his saddle back to the rodeo grounds but Tole said he'd be fine.

"Hey, look. I put your name down as my agent and manager. Wear this tag on your belt and you can get in to watch or you can get back to the contestant area. If I don't see you at the arena, I'll look for you at the beer tent," Tole said.

"Okay. See you tonight. Good luck."

oOo

On his way downtown, Lleyellyn stopped in at Highplains Haberdashery and bought a wide-brimmed straw hat so he'd fit in better. The sales lady asked him if he was in the rodeo.

"I'm just the agent for a saddle bronc rider. He's leading right now. I expect him to win tonight."

He thought the boots on display were too expensive.

"If you're looking for a good deal on boots, there's a sale rack in the back room."

He found a pair of Tony Lama Seconds in his size marked down to forty-nine ninety-nine.

"There's a ten-percent rodeo discount for professionals like yourself," the sales lady said, sealing the deal.

Walking to work with a new hat and a pair of the right kind of boots, Lleyellyn imagined he was getting some positive looks from people on the street. He began to feel like he belonged at the rodeo.

As he continued down Main Street, he passed the office of the Miles City Star. On a whim he suddenly stopped, turned back, and went inside.

"Can I help you?" a clerk behind the counter asked.

"I hope so. I'm the agent for Tole Winters. You had his picture on the front of the sports page this morning. I was wondering. Could I get a few glossy copies of that picture?"

"I think so. I'll be right back," the clerk said.

A young man, a year or two older him, emerged from a back room.

"We're one hundred percent digital. I can print you up some pictures. Two dollars a copy, black and white. Five dollars each in color. How many you want?"

Lleyellyn thought a moment. "Can I get ten black and white and four coloreds. That's what, forty bucks, right?"

"Plus tax. I'll have them in a few minutes."

After a short wait, he was handed a thick manila envelope. He checked the contents. Eight-by-ten glossies. They were sharper and bigger that the one in the paper. Tole appeared to be looking directly at the camera, a big smile on his face. Durango Sparky had all four feet in the air. The horse was looking at the camera as well. Tole's spurs were high on the horse's neck, his right hand raised in the air. It was, he thought, a spectacular action shot.

As he paid for the pictures, he asked the clerk, "Is the TV station's office around here?"

"Sure. Right through that door."

Lleyellyn went into the office of KATL.

"Help you?" the receptionist asked.

"I'd like to know if I can get a copy of any video your station took of the rodeo last night," he said.

"Probably. I'll have you talk to Erik. He handles that."

She picked up the phone.

"Erik, a gentleman here wants some dubs from last night's rodeo." She looked at Lleyellyn and smiled. "Go through that door there. Ask for Erik. Third door on the right."

He did as instructed. He stopped at the third office on the right. The door was open.

"Erik?"

"Yes. Come in. What dub you looking for?"

"I'd like to get a video of Tole Winters in the saddle bronc event last night. He's leading the event."

"We shot the whole rodeo. Three cameras simultaneously. Different angles. Let me check," he said, as he punched in some commands on the computer on his desk. "Yes. I can get you a dub from three angles. Start to finish. Will run about two or three minutes with the saddling up and the judging and all. You want VHS or DVD?"

"How much?" he asked.

"Fifteen for either. Twenty-five for both."

"I'll take 'em both."

oOo

Lleyellyn had less than an hour before he had to report to the beer tent.

Before heading back to the motel, he stopped by Big Sky Pharmacy and bought a Sharpie pen, then went around the corner to Wells Fargo where he deposited a hundred and seventy-five dollars of his beer tent earnings.

He got back to his motel room just as the maid was closing the door, a pile of sheets in her arms.

"Morning," he said.

"Buenas."

As he entered the room the phone was ringing. He picked it up.

"Hello."

"This is Max Fenton from the newspaper. Is this Tole Winters?"

Lleyellyn knew that this was the reporter who was doing the human interest piece on Tole. It was too much of an opportunity to miss. *Besides*, he thought, *I am his agent.*

"Yes. I'm Tole," he lied. "How can I help you?"

"I'm doing a piece about you for the paper. Since you're leading your event and all, our readers will be interested in learning a little about you."

Shay paused, then asked, "What do you want to know?"

"Well, first, some background. Hometown. School. That kind of stuff," the reporter said.

He didn't know much, but he decided to ad lib a little.

"I grew up on a little farm outside of Wilton, Wisconsin, near Tomah. We had cattle. Dairy mostly."

"Where did you go to school?"

"Right there in Wilton. Played sports. Mostly wrestling. Then I got into riding bucking horses and qualified for the National High School Rodeo just down the road from home in Tomah, Wisconsin."

"That where you won the high school championship?"

"Yes, sir. That's what got me thinking about this here pro rodeo event."

"How'd you learn how to ride bucking horses?"

He took his time. The story was coming together as he spoke.

"Just started riding, I guess. I watched a couple videos. How-to type of thing. And I read up on it a little, but mostly I learned by doing," he said.

"What about your family?"

"Well, my mom works in the Walmart office in Tomah. That's their distribution center. My dad has the farm and does Bob-cat and back-hoe work. I have three younger sisters. Still in school."

The reporter paused in his questioning. He could hear him typing on his keyboard.

Then the reporter said, "I met your agent last night. Kinda

young for an agent, isn't he?"

Lleyellyn cleared his throat and waited a few seconds before answering.

"You mean Lleyellyn Shay? We've been friends since the third grade. He's a smart guy. Good with numbers and with people. He handles my scheduling, travel arrangements, public relations, the whole bit. Makes my job a whole lot easier. He also handles the Tole Winters Fan Club. And he's working on my new web site."

Shay could hear the reporter's keys as he wrote down what he told him.

"What's he ... what's your agent know about rodeo?"

Lleyellyn didn't hesitate. The story was progressing smoothly.

"He was pretty good at riding stock. Bulls. Saddle broncs. Bareback. Got hurt and had to have some vertebrae fused together. Can't compete any more. When he did, though, he was way better 'n me."

Changing his tack, the reporter continued.

"How do you feel about the second round tonight?"

"Not bad. Good. My confidence is up. I just try and stay relaxed. Keep my focus. Try to last the eight seconds."

"What about your arm? Worried about that?" the reporter followed up.

"The doc said it's no big deal. I'll just keep my right arm up and out of the way, do my thing."

"Think your cast will affect your balance?"

"Shouldn't," Tole said, "but to tell you the truth, I've never ridden with a cast on before."

"Other riders tell me an arm in a cast can feel pretty weighty on the back of a bucking horse," the reporter said. "Good luck! Thanks for the info."

Shay hung up the phone. Before putting the photographs

and videos in a dresser drawer, he pulled out one of the colored pictures of Tole on Durango Shorty and wrote a message across the bottom with his new Sharpie. *For LaDonna Mae. Best Wishes. Your friend, Tole Winters.*

He walked across the street to the café. LaDonna Mae was sitting at a table near the back. The breakfast crowd had thinned out. She was counting her tips.

"Say, LaDonna Mae," he said as she looked up. "We wanted to give you a better picture than the one in the paper," he continued, as he handed it to her.

She took it and studied it for a moment.

"Thanks." She paused, and then asked, "You write this? Or did Tole?"

He paused, smiled, and said, "Let's just say it was professionally signed."

Then he turned and headed off for work.

oOo

Lleyellyn saw the banner across the beer tent as soon as he walked through the entrance gate.

WATCH THE RODEO HERE ON OUR FOUR BIG SCREEN TVS! Large black letters covered a ten-foot-long white banner atop the tent next to a Coors logo. There were a few men scattered in groups of two or three next to the four-sided bar. All four television sets were showing a local cooking show.

"What's with the TVs?" he asked his boss, who was busy tapping a keg.

"Local cable system hooked it up for us. Coors is paying for the feed. They can watch tonight's action in the comfort of the beer tent. Should draw a crowd."

"I don't see how it can get any busier than it was last night," Shay said, before moving to the other side of the tent, putting on an apron and filling the pockets with ten dollars in change. He realized immediately that he would be able to watch Tole's event when the action got going that evening.

By mid-afternoon business was brisk. The television was showing an Australian Rules football game which no one paid attention to.

At six, the boss told him to take a break and grab a bite to eat. He slipped under the bar and left the beer tent. He made sure Tole's official pass was visible hanging from his belt and joined the crowd heading to the grandstand. He strolled toward the Pass Gate where the attendant waived him through without a second glance.

Most of the people he saw looked like working rodeo cowboys. Many wore chaps and carried lariats or bridles. He didn't know a soul and he didn't see Tole.

Lleyellyn noticed a sign that said *LOCKER ROOM* above the door to a long white building behind the grandstand. He went inside. No one paid attention to him. Several men were busy putting on pads or wrapping their arms or other body parts. He saw Tole's saddle next to a locker and walked over just as Tole emerged from the wash room.

"Hey bud! What's up?" Tole said.

"Got a little break for a bite to eat. Just wanted to see how you're doing. What's with this bud crap?"

"Cowboy talk. Around here nobody says dude. That's a bad term. Nobody's hoss either. Everybody calls each other bud. Or pard. Pardner. Sometimes maybe Tex, or slim. It's a game they play. Pretty particular about it. Hell. There's a wrangler competing bareback they call Curley. Real name's on the roster. Blossom Curley. No one calls him Blossom, that's for damn sure."

"Well. Can I call you Tole?"

"Yeah, sure. You can always use a guy's nickname if you

know it." Then Tole paused, and said, "Whatever you do, don't call me Tolland. I'd have to turn in my pass. Leave town."

Tole said he'd probably be called for his ride about seven forty-five, eight o'clock.

"Think you can be here to watch it?" he asked.

"I'll see it for sure. They've set up a bunch of big TVs in the beer tent. Showing the action live. I'll have a better view than if I was in the front row."

Lleyellyn wished his friend good luck.

"They don't say break-a-leg in rodeo, do they?" he asked.

"Good luck will do. See you after the event," Tole said. "I'll look for you here or at the beer tent."

oOo

Shay had to squeeze through a closely-bunched crowd to even get up to the bar and then had to make a little room to stoop down and duck under the bar to report back to work. Orders came constantly and he was busy. He glanced up whenever possible to keep an eye on the action on one of the television screens.

He saw a part of the grand march and some barrel racing. It was busy during the calf-roping and he didn't see much. The crowd didn't seem much interested in the preliminary events.

After a commercial break, big printing on the screen announced: *Next event: Saddle Bronc Riding.* The crowd was loud and he couldn't hear the announcers. He picked up the remote and hit the close caption button. Printed words streamed across the bottom of the screen.

"Now it's time for the premier event. Miles City is known for bucking horse stock. Saddle Bronc Riding is the truest old time cowboy event."

The words continued to scroll across the screen with a little history of the event.

"Here's where it gets interesting. Top point getters tonight qualify for tomorrow's final go-round, and for a top prize of at least three thousand dollars. And leading is a newcomer. The current National High School Champion, Tole Winters, from Wilton, Wisconsin. Following him closely are three professional former national champions and some real up-and-comers. And, here's what makes it even more special, the livestock is absolutely the best. All top-ranked bucking-horses from right here in the bucking horse capital of the world. Miles City, Montana. U. S. A. Stay tuned for some real action. We'll be back in sixty seconds."

Shay glanced away and filled as many orders as he could. When the action came back on, the crowd seemed to grow quiet. Everyone was watching the action on the big screen. Lleyellyn kept watch and knew that Tole would be one of the last riders up. He glanced at the screen from time to time and then suddenly there he was. The TV showed a close-up of Tole standing behind the chute. He appeared relaxed. He was watching the action from behind the barricade. It looked like Tole had been doing this for years. He didn't look nervous. He appeared confident. Apparently noticing the camera, he looked right at it and grinned.

Man, I wish I could do that, Shay thought.

"Bartender! Two more Coors. I need a refill before the final feller. It's that Tole guy's turn," a lanky middle-aged man said. "Bet he don't make it."

"Here's your beer," Shay said. "Tole Winters will make it."

The man looked back at him, took a sip from his cup, and looked up at the screen.

"Well, we'll know soon enough."

The screen filled with the close-up face of Tole, then the camera backed away revealing Tole getting set on his horse. With the crowd suddenly quiet, Lleyellyn hit the remote and the sound returned.

"Young cowboy looks confident. The horse is a dandy. Out of the Circle M Ranch from near these parts. A mare. They're the tough ones. Simmer-On is her name."

Tole settled in, the little horse stood still, not touching the sides of the chute. Tole looked at the gate man, tugged his hat down, and nodded. Lleyellyn could read his lips.

"Let's do it!" Tole said, and then the gate swung open.

Simmer-On jumped out sideways with Tole raking his spurs immediately.

"Good start," the announcer said. "He qualified with the spurs. Let's see if the horse does its part."

Simmer-On bucked quickly three times in succession, its hind feet kicking back and up. Tole leaned back to keep his center of gravity, the white cast of his arm held high over his head.

"This cowboy busted his right arm last night, folks, but he's riding again tonight. That's the rodeo way."

The horse jumped sideways with all four feet in the air, then reared up on its hind legs.

"Folks, that cast must be getting mighty heavy. Lot of G-force when Simmer-On touches down. Cowboy's gotta keep from touching the horse. Or the reins. Or himself. We're at six seconds."

Lleyellyn was staring at Tole's cast. The white stood out brightly on the color screen. Tole seemed to be having a hard time holding his arm up. It seemed to come down a notch every time the horse bucked and landed.

"This is a good ride, folks! Good little horse. Winters is doing his part. Looks like a sure winner. There's the horn. I'm guessing eighty-nine, ninety on the score."

The crowd came alive. It seemed to think Tole had it won.

Lleyellyn glanced up at the screen. The crowd didn't notice at first, and then quieted again, quickly.

"Disqualified for letting his right hand touch his saddle or something. I didn't see it. Thought he made it. We'll have an instant replay in a minute," the announcer said.

The camera followed Tole as the pickup rider deftly helped him off Simmer-On. The little mare trotted back through the chute and Tole stepped down to the arena floor. He stood there with his hat in his hand. The crowd was whistling and booing. The disqualification was unpopular with the spectators.

"Here's a replay, folks. From several angles."

The screen showed the last two seconds of Tole's ride in slow motion from first the front, then the side and finally from overhead.

"Folks, judge for yourself. For the life of me, I just can't see where he touched anything with that right hand. His right arm stands out pretty good with that white cast and all. Maybe it attracted too much attention. Let's go down to the arena floor."

"This is Mattie Browning from Television Rodeo. Tole, what do you make of that DQ?"

Tole stood holding his hat in his right hand. He looked off to the crowd and gave a wave.

"I thought I made the time. I don't think I touched anything with my hand."

Then he paused.

"That was a right nice horse. Gave me all I could handle."

"Well," the reporter said, "what do you say when I tell you three instant replays show that you didn't touch anything. That you shouldn't have been DQ'd?"

Tole looked at Mattie Browning, then at his feet. Then he looked up and into the camera.

"Well, this is rodeo. Not the National Football League, you know. We don't have instant replays to over-rule the judges. The judges are just rodeo cowboys doing their best. I'm disappointed, sure. But that's rodeo."

The screen filled up with a beer commercial and Lleyellen poured a few. The middle-aged man who had bet Tole wouldn't make it caught his eye.

"Bud, that cowboy sure enough made it. If you was a betting man, you'd have won."

oOo

Shay kept a look-out for Tole as he helped keep the beer cups filled. By bartime the crowd was still five or six deep and he never saw Tole. As soon as the beer tent closed and they picked up the trash and stacked the empties, he hurried over to the locker room. Tole wasn't around. No one knew where he was. Shay figured he must have headed back to the motel.

oOo

The motel parking lot was full. Groups stood around the courtyard talking, laughing and drinking beer. He still didn't see Tole.

Lleyellen opened the door and entered the room. Tole was seated on the bed holding a towel to his shoulder.

"Man, you was robbed!" he said, entering the room. "What's the matter with your shoulder?"

"Shoulder hurts like hell. You're damned right I was robbed. I got robbed of the chance at two, three thousand bucks. And my darned shoulder hurts like a son-of-a-buck."

"What you doing with your shoulder?"

"Applying ice. Just like when I played football. Man, it was darned near impossible to hold my arm up when the horse kept bouncing up and down."

"Saw it all on TV," Lleyellyn said. "God, you looked great and the announcers thought you won. And then when you didn't, I thought you'd be pissed. I saw the interview on TV. Heard you say, 'well that's the rodeo,' or something. Sounded pretty professional. How you'd come up with that?"

Tole looked at him for a moment, then winced as he moved his arm and took a drink of water.

"When the pick-up man grabbed me he said, 'Son. Good job. Be professional,' or something. Then when the reporter started asking questions, I just thought back to some of those interviews you see on TV after some guy's been wrecked in a NASCAR race."

"You mean, like, 'I wanna thank Pennzoil, Hardees and Safeway Foods, the car was handling great. We had her set up just right. We were headed for a top ten finish sure. But that's racing. We'll be back next week in the Pennzoil, Hardees, Safeway Foods, Sans-a-belt, Viagra Special'?"

"You got that right. Like when the guy's in last place and gets spun out on purpose," Tole replied.

Shay sat there looking at his friend.

"Think you should have that shoulder looked at again? How's it feel?"

Tole tried to move his arm. Lou Ellen could tell Tole was in pain.

"My shoulder hurts all the time. When I move it's really bad. Whole arm doesn't feel right."

CHAPTER SIX

May 19

They stayed in the room and watched the rodeo on television. Lleyellyn thought Tole would be interested in the saddle bronc finals, but he didn't pay much attention to it. Shay went out and picked up a pizza. He was hungry but Tole had only a bite or two.

About six that afternoon, he said, "My arm is throbbing real bad. Pain pills aren't much help. I don't think I can sleep. Sure not hungry, or anything."

"Let's go back to the infirmary. Check out your arm. Maybe they can give you something. Pain pill, maybe."

"I don't think I want to walk that far," Tole said.

"I'll get us a ride," Shay said and left the room.

Five minutes later he was back.

"Feller out here said he'll give us a ride. He's a calf-roper."

The rodeo grounds were nearly deserted. Two stock trucks were pulling out and the beer tent was dark. The calf-roper pulled right up to the infirmary in his F-250 and Lleyellyn jumped out. The door was locked. A hand-lettered sign on the glass door said it all.

INFIRMARY CLOSED.
SEE YOU AT THE PENDLETON RODEO

*CONTACT THE LOCAL EMERGENCY ROOM
OR WALK-IN CLINIC.
IN AN EMERGENCY CALL 911*

"Damn thing's closed," he said climbing back in the truck. "Can you take us to the hospital?"

oOo

The lady behind the counter asked, "What can I do for you boys?"

Tole stepped forward.

"I hurt my shoulder tonight at the rodeo. Like to get my shoulder and my cast, my arm, checked out."

"Insurance card, please."

"Ma'am, I don't have insurance. The infirmary at the rodeo said to stop in here if there are any problems," Tole said.

The lady looked up from her desk and gave a brief half-smile.

"The infirmary is operated by the rodeo. First aid station, really. This hospital has nothing to do with the rodeo. Did you buy the PRA insurance when you paid your entry fee?"

"No, Ma'am. Not that I know of. My uncle paid the entry fee. This was my first rodeo. I don't think I have insurance," Tole said.

"We'll have to take care of the financial arrangements before I can let you see the doctor. Fill out this form. I'll need five hundred dollars up front to get you started. Should cover a shoulder x-ray and examination. After that, we'll have to see what the doctor says."

"But, Ma'am..." Tole started, until Lleyellyn interrupted.

"Tole, let's sit over here. I can help you fill out that form," he said, leading the way to the little alcove that served as the ER waiting area.

"I can use my cash card. Pretty much wipe me out, though."

"Look. You need the help. I've got a little over three hundred in cash on me. Good night at the beer tent. You have any cash?"

"Maybe hundred fifty, or so. Not exactly sure," Tole said.

"Well, let's count it up."

Lleyellen took out his wallet and counted out three hundred and twenty-four dollars. Tole pulled a wad of bills from the left front pocket of his jeans and tried to count them out one-handed.

"Let me help you there," Lleyellen said as he took the roll and carefully counted out one hundred and fourteen dollars in assorted bills.

"What do we have?" he said. "Four hundred thirty-eight, right?"

"Yeah. That's what I get. Short sixty-two bucks," Tole said.

Lleyellyn didn't say anything, but took off his right boot. He reached inside and removed several bills that were folded in half.

"I've got this hundred bucks of walking-around money. We got more than enough."

Tole returned to the counter.

"Here's the form, ma'am. And the money."

"Take a seat. The doctor will see you in a few minutes."

No one else was around. The waiting room was empty. The clock said three forty-one. It had been a long day.

"I'll pay you back from my bank account," Tole said.

"Don't worry. We'll settle up later. I'm more worried about your arm. And shoulder."

"With this ER bill and my entry fee and travel expenses, saddle bronc riding hasn't paid off too well, has it?" Tole said. "Looks like I'm at least a thousand bucks in the hole. How'd you do at the beer tent tonight?"

Lleyellyn glanced up at Tole and then heard the doctor say, "Mr. Winters? I'll see you now."

"I'll tell you later. Want me to stay out here?"

"Hell no. Come on in. You're my agent. Earn your money," Tole said.

oOo

The doctor examined Tole's arm and immediately ordered that the cast be cut off.

"Your arm's swollen. Good thing you came in tonight."

Then he sent Tole down the hall for x-rays of his arm and shoulder while he answered a phone call.

When the doctor came back to the examination room he had two x-rays in his hand.

"First the good news," he said. "The alignment of your fracture is still good. I was afraid waving it around might have done something, but it seems okay. No internal bleeding around the break, either." Tole glanced at Lleyellyn, who smiled back.

"What's the bad news?"

"Well, look at this image of your shoulder. All that back and forth, up and down motion while you were on horseback being bucked around seems to have caused some damage. The cast was heavy. The torque caused by the bucking horse was extreme. If you were a baseball pitcher I'd tell you about rotator-cuff injuries. What you need to do is rest that shoulder, apply ice packs, get the swelling down, and then we'll see how it is. Riding a bucking animal of any kind with a cast on your arm was contraindicated. By that I mean, you shouldn't have done it," the doctor said.

"But the doc at the infirmary said it would be okay." Tole said.

The doctor stepped back and looked at Tole.

"Son, rodeo doctors are sort of like the doctors you see at

prize fights. Their job is to keep the audience happy. The fracture is no big deal. The shoulder, well, that's yet to be determined. You'll need to rest it for a while. And just so I make myself clear, no bucking horses, no dirt bikes, nothing like that, not until you're fully healed."

Just before they left the Emergency Room, the doctor handed Tole a small vial of pills.

"I'm giving you some pain medication. Samples. Take one if the pain gets too bad. When the swelling starts to go down, the pain should decrease. And here's a prescription in case you need a refill."

"Thanks."

"I want you to come back in about two weeks so I can see how things are. Both the fracture and the shoulder will need looking at. Okay?"

"Sure. Right," Tole said.

The hospital parking lot was nearly empty.

"Let's walk," Tole said. "I haven't seen a taxi in this town since we got here."

"Only five or six blocks," Lleyellyn said.

They started out, neither of them saying anything. Finally Tole broke the silence.

"I'm really pissed. I won the event. The chance at the top prize should have been mine."

"Yeah. You was robbed. The people watching it on TV around me all thought you got hosed. So did the announcers. So did I."

"I've got a broken arm, bunged up shoulder, and I owe you, what, four hundred dollars, right?"

"Not that much. Don't worry about it. We can settle up later."

"Well, here I am, the great bronc rider, and I end up injured and in the hole about a grand."

Then Tole stopped, looked at his friend, and continued, "What about you? How'd it go selling beer tonight?"

Shay looked away momentarily. He was embarrassed. Then he said, "Better 'n last night. Made a little over three hundred. Pretty good tips. Almost six hundred for the two nights."

"No bull!" Tole said. "It doesn't take a genius to see that selling beer was a whole lot better than riding bucking horses."

"Well, you got some great publicity. Good stuff on TV. The crowd seemed to like you."

"Maybe so. But being Mr. Big in Miles City doesn't seem like much. The rodeo will be over for the year. I can't ride tomorrow. Not until I heal up. Who knows how long that will be. It's a friggin' son-of-a-bitch."

They walked in silence again for nearly a block.

"You know, a reporter called me when you were gone yesterday. Wanted some background for a story he's doing about you. Probably in tomorrow's Sunday paper," Shay said.

"Yeah. What'd you tell him?"

"I can't remember all the stuff. Some I sort of guessed at. Did your mother ever work at the Walmart district office?"

"No. Why?" Tole asked.

"Just wondering. Your dad operate a back-hoe?"

"Heck no. My dad died when I was six. He was an accountant. My ma's been in a nursing home for years. Stroke. Why?" Tole asked.

"I think the reporter had it all wrong," Lleyellyn said. "Wonder where he got his facts."

oOo

Shay was the first one awake. He pulled on his pants, grabbed his billfold and walked down to the motel office.

"I need some quarters for a paper," he told the clerk.

He fed six quarters into the slot and got a paper. The top of the front page had a teaser above the mast head: *HIGH SCHOOL CHAMP DQed ON JUDGES' ERROR*, it read. *See Section C, Page 1.*

He threw the Sunday advertising sections in the trash can, then extracted section C from the news sections. On the first page, filling a third of the page, was a picture of Tole, waving his hat in the air and smiling at the crowd. It was taken a split-second before he realized he'd been disqualified. He hurried back to the room looking through the paper as he did so.

Section C was wholly devoted to the rodeo. Under the big close-up picture of Tole was the caption: *HIGH SCHOOL CHAMP DISQUALIFIED IN BUCKING HORSE EVENT ON JUDGES' ERROR – DENIED CHANCE AT FIRST PRIZE.*

The featured article re-capped the final results for all the events. A column on the left side of the page was devoted to Tole Winters. *NEWCOMER TOLE WINTERS*, the heading read.

Lleyellyn scanned the story. It was all there. The background he had invented. Tole's home town, his parents' jobs, and everything else he'd made up. There was mention of Winter's young agent-manager, Lleyellyn Shay, a former bull-rider with several fused vertebra to show for it and mention of the Tole Winter Fan Club and web site.

I wonder what Tole will think about this, he thought as he approached the motel room. *He sure got a lot of press.*

As he entered the room, Tole was just finishing buttoning his shirt.

"Man, I'm feeling a whole lot better. Can you give me a hand here? Buttons are tough one-handed."

"Sure," Lleyellyn said, laying the paper on the bed and helping with the buttons. "You made the paper big time," he said, picking up the rodeo section. "Look at this."

Tole took the paper and looked at it. A smile formed at his mouth.

"Holy cow! Pretty big picture."

"There's an article just about you with some background. The main story says everyone agrees the judges screwed up. You should've won."

Shay watched as Tole read the main article.

"Yeah, great. But they can't change the results. Doesn't mention my shoulder, though, does it?"

He didn't answer, but continued watching as Tole read the personal interest column.

"Gee, my ma never worked at Walmart and my dad sure never had dairy cattle or operated a back-hoe or a Bob-cat," Tole said, then read some more. "You! I know you've never ridden a bull or had back surgery," he added. Tole looked up from the paper. "This is all stuff you told the reporter, isn't it?"

Lleyellyn just smiled.

"Well," Tole said, "I think that agent stuff's gone to your head, but heck, I like it. It's way better'n than my ma's in a facility and my dad's been dead since I was little."

"I was just trying to help you get some publicity. I was worried you might be pissed off."

"Heck no," Tole said.

Tole folded the paper and put it on the dresser next to the TV.

"I'm hungry. Let's go over and grab some breakfast."

As soon as they walked into the café, several people looked up. Lleyellyn could tell they recognized Tole.

On the wall behind the cash register was the color photograph of Tole on Durango Shorty that Lleyellyn had signed for the waitress. Someone had had it framed. He knew Tole saw the picture.

"Lleyellyn, where'd you get the photo?"

"Newspaper office. Part of an agent's job. I've got some extra copies back in the room."

The swinging door from the kitchen swung open just then, and LaDonna Mae came out carrying a tray full of breakfast plates. She saw them immediately, and smiled.

"Morning Lleyellyn. Morning Tole. Take that booth over by the window."

After they were seated, La Donna Mae approached their table, order pad open and pencil poised.

"Tole, you were robbed. You won the event fair and square," she said. "How's your arm and all?"

Tole smiled back.

Shay said, "His arm's a little sore. Needs some rest. Did you watch the rodeo?"

LaDonna Mae made eye contact with both of them.

"I watched it from the beer tent. On TV. I saw you there, Lleyellyn, but you were so busy I didn't want to interrupt you." Then she smiled broadly. "I didn't realize agents had to bartend, too."

"Mine does. Can't make much being the agent for a non-qualifier. Somebody's gotta pay the bills, right, Lleyellyn?"

"I guess."

LaDonna Mae was silent as she picked up the tip left by the previous customer.

"One coffee. One Mountain Dew. Right?"

The waitress brought their drinks and they ordered breakfast. She delivered their platters a few minutes later.

"Put that ham over here, will you, LaDonna Mae?" Shay said. "I've gotta cut it up a little for Tole. Hard for him to do one-handed."

While they were eating, two kids about ten asked Tole to autograph the picture they had cut from the Sunday paper. Lleyellyn helped with that, too.

"Thanks, Mr. Winters," one of them said.

"No problem. You're welcome. Call me Tole."

oOo

When they finished eating, Tole went to the men's room. LaDonna Mae came over to Lleyellyn.

"You don't know it, but you met my daddy last night," she said.

"I did?" Lleyellyn said, thinking who that could be, the doctor, the calf-roper, somebody in the locker room. "I don't know who that could be."

"I pointed you out to him when I was at the beer tent and you was real busy. He said you and him talked about whether or not Tole would make the time," LaDonna Mae said.

"Oh, yeah. Tall, slim guy. Nice Stetson. Seems I remember him. Nice guy."

"Well, my daddy always throws a party on the day after the rodeo's over. You're invited. You and Tole. Starts about two in the afternoon. Lots of good food. Drinks. Everything. Can you come?"

He was about to answer when Tole came back.

"Hey pard," he said, "I just wrangled us an invite to a party. This afternoon. LaDonna Mae's daddy's throwing it."

"Great," Tole said.

"We'll be there," Shay said. "How do we get there?"

"I'll draw you a little map," LaDonna Mae said, and picked up the bill and sketched the directions on the back.

"Here. About a mile out of town on County Road R. Phone number's there if you get lost," she said, handing the paper to Lleyellyn. "And breakfast's on the house."

They watched her as she walked away. Then she abruptly stopped and came back.

Lleyellyn thought she would say something about him watching her backside as she walked away, but instead she smiled and asked, "Do you have a vehicle?"

He cleared his throat.

"No. We came in by van. Can we walk to your place?"

"You're staying across the street at the motel, right?"

He nodded.

"I'll have my brother pick you up at two. What room?"

He gave her the room number and she jotted it down on the back of her order pad.

"See you this afternoon," she said, and then turned and walked toward the kitchen, Shay following her with his eyes.

As he watched, she gave her hips an extra flounce and he knew it was for his benefit. His face reddened. He glanced up at Tole who was staring back at him with a slight smile. He didn't say anything. He just winked.

oOo

LaDonna Mae's brother pulled up in front of room six at quarter past two. They heard the truck.

They went outside.

"Hey! I'm La Donna Mae's brother. You guys Tole and Lleyellyn?"

"I'm Tole. He's Lleyellyn."

"Glad to meet you," Lleyellyn said, shaking hands. "What's your name?"

"Jimmy. Jimmy Ritchie," he said, shaking Tole's hand as well. "Hop in. You'll like the party."

They both climbed into the front seat, Shay in the middle.

"Nice truck," he said. "Yours?"

"You bet. Seventy-nine Ford. F-150. I fixed it up in auto-shop at school and at home. My dad helped me some," Jimmy said. "It'll do ninety, a hundred, easy."

"How old are you?" Lleyellyn asked.

"Sixteen. Got my driver's license two years ago."

Jimmy turned out onto the highway and headed north.

"Our place is just up the road a little ways and across the section-line road."

Ahead, they could see a set of buildings set back from the road in the middle of a grove of trees. The long driveway was lined with parked vehicles. As they got closer, they could see that they were nearly all pickups.

"I'm going to drive all the way back to the barn. Then I'll introduce you around," Jimmy said.

The yard was full of people. Little kids were crowded around a tire swing suspended from a tall cottonwood. Under a white screen-sided tent a long table was set up. Several women were arranging potluck bowls and dishes.

There were more than a dozen men in broad-brimmed hats congregated around a shiny new-looking galvanized-steel stock tank filled to overflowing with cans of beer and chunks of ice. Other people were going in and out of the house, and the chairs on the big front porch were all occupied. Women with babies and older couples were in groups in the shade sharing the news.

"LaDonna Mae's around somewhere," Jimmy said. "Grab a beer and I'll introduce you around."

They walked over to the beer tank.

"Hey guys," Jimmy said, "this here's Tole Winters, the bronc rider who got cheated out of the big prize last night, and his friend Lleyellyn."

Several people howdied welcomes and someone handed them each a beer. A guy about their age stepped forward.

"I was there last night. Damn good ride. You got screwed," he said, looking at Tole.

"Well thanks," Tole said. "That's rodeo."

"You got that right," someone else chimed in before spitting a stream of tobacco to one side.

They both stood there making small talk. After a few

minutes, a lanky middle-aged man stepped over to Tole.

"I'm Dan Lassen. I saw your event last night, too. Darn good job," he said.

Tole just smiled.

"There's a guy over here you should meet. Spent a dozen years on the pro-rodeo circuit. Went to the National Finals Rodeo in Las Vegas several times. Was in the top ten for the All-Around Cowboy title one year."

They both walked over with Lassen toward the row of pickups, Shay trailing a little behind.

"Buck," Lassen said, approaching a man leaning on a cane and resting against a front fender of a green Dodge extended cab pickup. "This is the new saddle bronc rider that almost won last night."

Buck was about fifty, Lleyellyn supposed. Slight build. Curley black hair starting to go gray at the temples.

First Tole, then Shay shook hands with Buck.

"Buck," Lassen said, "got any advice for this aspiring bronc buster?"

Buck looked at Tole, then placed a Lucky between his lips and ignited it with a Zippo. He took a puff, squinted in the acrid smoke, and smiled.

"Rodeo was my whole life," he said. "I made it pretty far up the ladder. Just missed a top-ten at the national finals. Made some money. Got a lot of pretty good pussy. Broke twenty-seven different bones. Ribs. Both collar bones. Arms."

He paused, and took a long drag on his cigarette.

"You know, there's three bones in each arm. That's six, altogether," he paused again. Smiled. "I've broken five of the six. One three times. Concussions. Teeth. Knees. When I finally crashed for good I didn't have much to show for it. A pickup I owed more on than it was worth. A box of buckles I won as prizes over the years. No woman. No house. Really not much to show for my successful rodeo career."

"Then why'd you do it?" Tole asked.

Buck looked down at his boots. He slowly shook his head, then looked up, glancing at each of them in turn.

"Rodeo was what I always wanted to do. Always thought I'd make it big. Medical bills always added up to more than the prize money. Sponsors didn't cover the costs. I love the crowds. But, shit, I'm now forty-two, a has-been. No one gives a shit about me anymore."

Lleyellyn wanted to say something, but didn't know how to begin. Tole took off his hat and scratched the top of his head thoughtfully. Buck interrupted their thoughts.

"Boys, I hate to admit it, but let me tell you this. When I got out of high school, my best friend and I decided to rodeo. He was better than me. We both competed at Rawlins that first summer. Both of us did okay. He quit the rodeo right after that and I kept on going. I'm now a middle-aged cripple with no real job. I drive a cattle truck whenever I can. My buddy, he went home and started at the feed mill. Got married. Had kids. Now he's the manager with an ownership interest. Nice house. Nice wife. Daughter about to start college. Summer place on a lake. Made the right choice," Buck said. "I sure enough didn't."

Tole had some questions and Shay got out of their way and let them talk. He joined a group of men standing in a loose line before a *Johnny on the Spot* marked *MEN*.

Everyone seemed to be holding a can of beer and having a good time joking and razzing each other. Talking trash.

"Hey! Steve," the guy in front of Lleyellyn shouted to someone at the head of the line. "Find the woman of your dreams yet?"

Steve turned around. "You mean the retired stripper that owns a liquor store?"

"Yeah. And a nymphomaniac, to boot," the guy in front of

Lleyellyn replied, paraphrasing an old joke.

The whole line was laughing, eager to see what Steve would say to this, when the door of a nearby portable toilet marked *LADIES* banged open and LaDonna Mae stepped out.

"You numbskulls haven't changed since junior high," she said, addressing them all. "In ten years you'll all be lucky if you're living in house trailers in Missoula or somewhere, washing dishes, changing diapers and watching a lot of TV," she said, and started to stride off.

Steve shouted after her, "Hey wait! We were just joking. What kind of a guy are you going to marry, LaDonna Mae Ritchie?"

LaDonna Mae turned around.

"Oh, I don't know. A guy with ten thousand acres. Nice house. Clean. Polite. Respectful. And owns his own candy store." She smiled. "My goals are on a higher plane than any of yours, that's for sure."

As she walked away, Shay heard several men agree that LaDonna Mae was a real spit-fire.

"She's a cute little thing, but head-strong. Spirited," someone said.

When he left the porta-potty after finishing his business, Lleyellyn looked around. He didn't see Tole. He started back to get another beer, when he heard a voice behind him.

"Glad you made it." It was LaDonna Mae.

"Hey, I'm real sorry..." he started, before she cut him off.

"Those guys have been retreading the same old tire for years. I've got someone I want you to meet.

"Daddy, I'd like to introduce my friend, Lleyellyn. You talked to him last night."

"Lleyellyn," her father said, "yes, I remember. We met last night. You're the agent for the young bronc rider, right?"

"Yes, sir." They shook hands.

"Well, make yourself to home. LaDonna Mae will show you around. Lots of good food. Don't leave hungry."

"No, sir. I sure won't," Lleyellyn said, as LaDonna Mae grabbed his arm.

"There's other people you have to meet."

They walked around to the side of the house.

"I've got to ask you something," she said.

"Ask away."

"What are you and Tole going to do now? I mean, Tole can't compete for quite a while," she said.

"I'm not sure. Tole and me haven't discussed it much. I started out less than a week ago on my way to Portland, Oregon. I got off here on a whim, really."

"You still going there?"

"Don't know. Maybe."

"You guys have been friends since what, the third grade?" LaDonna Mae said.

Lleyellyn looked away a moment thinking about what to say. *She must have read the story in the morning's paper.*

"LaDonna Mae, you can't believe everything you read in the newspaper. I met Tole on the Amtrak. Few days ago. Paper's got it wrong," he said.

LaDonna Mae looked at him, a small frown furrowing her forehead.

"I don't know anything about you then, do I?" she said.

"Hey," Lleyellyn said, putting his hand over hers. "I'll tell you what you want to know. Might take a while. Pretty boring stuff," he said, then smiled. "I'd like to find more out about you, too."

oOo

From the porch he saw Tole standing with a circle of men about their age. Tole seemed to be the center of attention. He walked toward the group.

Tole looked up. "Here's my agent," Tole said, nodding toward Lleyellyn, by way of introduction.

"Ex-bull rider, right?" someone said.

"You bet. Before I wrecked. Not what you'd call a real success," Shay said, continuing the lie he had started a day earlier.

When the group went on to another topic, Lleyellyn whispered to Tole, "Think I'll head back. You staying?"

"Yeah. I'll catch a ride. See you at the motel."

Lleyellyn looked around and saw LaDonna Mae filling a plate in the white tent. He walked over.

"I'm heading back to the motel. See you tomorrow."

LaDonna Mae looked at him, then placed her plate on the table.

"Wait! Just wait. Eat something. Then I'll drive you."

oOo

She was a good driver, keeping her eyes on the road, glancing at him from time to time. They didn't say much to each other. She kept under the speed limit.

"I enjoyed the party, but I kind of felt out of place with all the real cowboys and such," he finally said. "You're about the only one I really wanted to talk to."

She didn't reply at first, then reached to turn on the radio, but stopped and said, "This'll give us a chance to talk. You can tell me about you and I'll tell you a little bit about me. So we can learn about each other."

He didn't know what to say to her. She didn't say anything either, apparently concentrating on driving. He enjoyed her company. As they entered Miles City she slowed and followed a steady stream of traffic until they reached the motel. She drove up to his door and looked at him.

"Thanks," he said, then he leaned over and gave her a kiss on the lips. She placed a hand on his shoulder and returned the kiss. They stared at each other for a moment before Lleyellyn broke the silence.

"Why don't you come in for a while. We can talk some."

He was sure she'd decline the offer, but she surprised him when she said, "Okay. You get out. I'm going to park around back. I don't want anyone from the restaurant seeing my truck. They'll get ideas and start talking. Don't lock the door."

Lleyellyn turned on the light and looked around. The maid had cleaned the room. The bed was made and the wastebaskets emptied. He put his spare clothes in a dresser drawer and checked out the bathroom. It had been cleaned. Fresh towels. For some reason, he put the toilet seat down.

He was waiting just inside the door when LaDonna Mae opened it, entered and closed it behind her and threw her purse on the nearest bed.

Then she walked up to him, put her hands around his waist, and gave him another kiss. He squeezed her hard against him, unsure what to do next.

"Shall we talk now, or later?" she said.

Before he could answer, she walked over to his bed, turned down the bedspread and turned to face him, her head cocked inquisitively.

He cleared his throat, and said, "Maybe later."

LaDonna Mae, without another word, pulled her dress over her head, unfastened her bra and pulled down her panties. In two or three seconds she was standing naked before him.

"Haven't you seen freckles before?" she asked, smiling. "Quit staring."

"It's not your freckles I'm looking at," he said.

CHAPTER SEVEN

May 20

The sheets were in disarray. They felt damp. Lleyellyn felt a chill as his perspiration evaporated. LaDonna Mae slid over closer to him and pulled a sheet up over the two of them.

"I'm glad I came," she said before they both burst out laughing from the unintended double entendre.

He started to doze off.

"I think I better get out of here before Tole shows up," LaDonna Mae said.

"Didn't realize it was getting so late."

He helped her round up her clothes which she took into the bathroom to get dressed. She came out in a few minutes.

"Lou Ellen, my oh my. We can always talk next time."

She was out the door before he could reply.

oOo

Tole opened the motel room door a little after two. He went to the bathroom. Shay could hear him urinating, then the splash of water in the basin.

"How was the rest of the party?" he asked.

"Pretty much the same. I spent a lot of time talking to Buck," Tole said.

"You mean the broken-down ex-cowboy?" Lleyellyn said.

"You got it. But he was big time. Had his shot. It cost him his health."

Lleyellyn looked at him. He had never seen him so serious.

"My mind's pretty much made up," Tole said. "The risk isn't worth the reward. Your way is way better."

"What do you mean?"

"Working a real job. Tend bar maybe. Lot better future than what I've been up to," Tole said.

He didn't say anything. He turned over as Tole turned out the light.

"See you in the morning."

oOo

"I don't have to stay around here," Tole said, almost before Lleyellyn had his eyes open. "Let's both go out to Oregon. I can get my arm checked anywhere."

"There might be a job around here," Shay said.

"You can get a job anywhere if you're willing to work. I can, too, once my arm's better."

"Okay. So what are you saying?"

"Let's go to Portland. Look for work. Start over," Tole said.

"Take the train?"

"Hell no. Let's save what little money we have. Hitch hike."

"It's a long way to go."

"I don't think we'll have any trouble. People are suckers for cowboys. You can tote my saddle and we'll wear our cowboy hats. We'll get a ride in no time."

oOo

The phone rang as they were getting ready to cross the street to the café and grab breakfast. Tole picked up the phone, said, "Hello," and listened.

"Sure. Where's your place?" he said, and listened some more.

"Okay. I'll be there in a bit. Okay if I bring my friend, Lleyellyn?"

When the conversation was finished, Tole hung up the phone and turned toward Shay.

"That was Buck. Remember? The old rodeo hand I talked to yesterday. He wants us to stop by his place."

"You sure you want me along?"

"You bet. We can go now. He lives just past the feed store and across the tracks."

They approached Buck's place, a vintage single-wide on cement blocks. A rusted older pickup was parked in the front yard, one wheel missing, the truck balancing on a bumper jack. Three mounted snow tires leaned against the trailer next to a dented overflowing trash barrel. The screen door was ajar, the front door open.

Tole stepped up to the door. Before he could knock, they heard Buck shout, "Come on in! Door's open."

They entered the trailer letting their eyes adjust to the dim light. Shay looked around. The room was surprisingly neat.

"Pour yourselves some coffee. There's biscuits on the stove. Help yourself," Buck said.

When they were both settled on stiff-backed kitchen chairs facing Buck seated on the only upholstered chair in the room, Buck leaned back, glanced briefly at Lleyellyn, and directed his gaze toward Tole.

"Reason I asked you over, Tole, was to apologize for the

way I carried on yesterday. Rodeo hasn't worked out for me. Might be different for you."

Tole looked at the ceiling, drank a little coffee and took a bite of biscuit.

"Last night I thought about what you said. Made sense to me. I don't really have much of a background in riding bucking horses. I've never even been, you know, just plain horseback riding. And I haven't ridden more than about twenty, twenty-five bucking horses in my whole lifetime. Just got started last fall. Sort of on a dare."

"Well, you fooled me," Buck said. "You seem to have some talent for it."

"I didn't realize how dangerous it was. How much luck is involved. Good luck, and bad."

Lleyellyn sat there listening. He realized that Tole had made his decision. His mind was made up.

"Think I'll start college. Get a job. What you said about your friend who left the rodeo to get married and start a career made more sense than I would have admitted a week ago," Tole said.

"Well, just don't base everything on me. You could get a second opinion, you know."

"Sure. I know," Tole said. "But I think I've decided to go straight."

The three of them sat there silently for a while, before Buck continued.

"Hey! I've got something for you boys. Could you hand me that box over there on the shelf?"

Shay stood up and walked over to an open bookcase. He picked up a wooden cartridge box and carried it back to Buck. He could see it was filled with buckles. It was heavier than it looked.

"These are the buckles I was telling you about yesterday."

he said, looking at Tole. "They give these out as prizes at most rodeos. At least they used to. I want to give you one. To each of you," Buck added, glancing at Lleyellyn.

He reached in and picked up and looked at several different buckles.

"See this one? Bucking horse. Says Elko, Nevada across here," he said pointing. "Hand me that polishing rag there, will you?"

Lleyellyn did.

"You don't want to shine 'em up too good. Just polish the parts that stick out. Makes it look like you use it all the time."

Buck finished polishing and held out the buckle.

"Here, Tole, a little remembrance from me."

Tole started to speak. Buck cut him off.

"I want you to take it." He handed it over. "I remember I won the bare-back event that week. Went out and got really drunk. Elko is a great party town. Real old-time cowboy place. I woke up next to this little red-head said she was from Amarillo. Barrel racer, I think. Never saw her again. A few days later I found out I had the clap. Used up the better part of my prize money on penicillin. I'm not sure if that was a rodeo injury or not," Buck said, suppressing a laugh. "That was one of my better days."

"Thanks, Buck," Tole said as he slipped off his belt and replaced his store-bought buckle. As he threaded his belt through the loops on his jeans, he added, "I'll wear it all the time."

Shay watched Buck rummage around in the box and inspect several other buckles.

"Lleyellyn, here's one for you. Got this big bull's head. Rode bulls for the money. Some. Won this one in Cheyenne. Won, and broke my danged leg on the dismount."

He took the buckle and hefted it. It was heavier than he thought it would be.

"Thanks," he said, and started to fasten it to his belt while Tole picked up the box and put it back on the shelf.

"I gave you that because I heard you used to ride bulls."

Lleyellyn looked down at the floor, then sheepishly back at Buck.

"No, sir. I've never rode anything. I'm just helping out Tole here. He calls me his agent."

"Well, that's a good thing," Buck said. "Can't break too many bones in the agent business."

Buck offered them more coffee and they small-talked a while longer.

When they were ready to leave, Buck said, "Thanks for stopping by. Good luck with whatever you men decide to do."

oOo

They walked home. Just before they reached the motel, Tole said, "I've decided to head back to my uncle's place. Heal up. Go back to school."

Lleyellyn didn't reply but considered Tole's decision.

As they entered the motel room, Tole spoke again.

"Got any of those pictures like you left at the café? I want to send one to my uncle when I tell him I'm coming home."

"Sure. You want black and white or full color? Your choice." Lleyellyn said as held out one of each. "And here's a Sharpie if you want to autograph it."

Tole flashed a broad smile. "You're my agent," Tole said. "Autographing's your job."

"What shall I put?"

"You decide," Tole said, handing the pen back.

Llelleyn thought, a slight furrow appearing between his eyebrows, then wrote, *"Unk, Thanks for everything. Love, Tolland 'Tole' Winters."*

Tole looked at it. Lleyellyn could see a slight smile forming on Tole's lips.

"Okay," he said. "My sentiments exactly."

CHAPTER EIGHT

May 21

Tole's ride was due any minute. One of the guys he had met at the party was taking him to Havre, Montana so he could catch the Amtrak back to Wisconsin.

"Look," Tole said. "I still owe you some money from the hospital. Take my saddle. Try and sell it. Keep what I owe you, and your agent's cut. You can send me the rest, if there's any."

"Hell, man, keep your saddle. You can settle up some other time. I'm not worried."

"No," Tole replied. "I thought about it last night. I've had my fill of rodeo. I need to make some important decisions. Look, the saddle cost just under two thousand dollars new. Used, worth maybe half that. Less probably. You might be able to get seven hundred, maybe a little more. Enough to settle up with and a little left over. Do what you can with it."

Tole handed him a slip of paper.

"You can reach me here, at least until I find out if I'm going to college this fall or not."

Llelleyn wasn't sure what to say. Just then they heard a truck pull up outside.

"That's my ride," Tole said. "Hey, before I go, I just want to thank you for all the help you gave me. I consider us best friends. Anything time you need anything I'll be there for you. I mean it. I owe you."

Lleyellyn followed him outside, thinking about what Tole had just said. They shook hands, then surprised themselves by hugging each other. Tole threw his bag in back of the truck and climbed in. He looked over at his friend and gave him a thumbs up as the truck pulled away.

Shay watched it turn onto the highway. He couldn't believe it. Less than two short weeks. A lot had happened. Made a real friend in Tole. LaDonna Mae, too, he hoped. The rodeo. A fresh start. A whole panorama of recent unexpected surprises were jumbled up in his mind.

"Now," he thought, "what am I gonna do?"

oOo

Before checking out of the motel, Shay called the two tack dealers listed in the phone book. Neither was interested in buying a used rodeo saddle.

"Come back closer to rodeo time," one said. "Might be a little more demand then."

He entered the motel office with his duffel bag in one hand and the saddle slung over his shoulder.

"I'm checking out. Here's the key." he said.

The clerk checked his records.

"All set. Your buddy, the cowboy, paid the bill last night."

He wasn't surprised, although Tole hadn't mentioned paying the bill.

I never got a chance to thank him.

oOo

So far, Tole's theory about a cowboy not having to wait long to catch a ride wasn't holding true.

He stood just past the last gas station on the road out of town heading south. He was wearing the broad-rimmed cowboy hat he had bought a few days earlier, the big buckle Buck had given him, his bargain priced high-heeled boots and his other gear. His duffel bag and the saddle were at his feet, in prominent view of approaching cars.

Grass and grain fields stretched to the horizon. There was no traffic in sight. Two crows called to each other from adjoining telephone poles.

Occasionally a vehicle passed headed into town. One or two pickups passed without even slowing down. The drivers didn't glance his way. Three high school kids roared past, one of them shouting, "Get a horse!"

As usual there was a steady wind, but it was sunny and comfortable. Time passed slowly. He was still hopeful, but hitching a ride wasn't as easy as they had imagined. He noticed a big blue Dodge pickup towing an aluminum stock trailer pull out of the gas station on the edge of town and head his way. Before he could even raise his thumb to signal for a ride, the truck slowed and stopped next to him in the middle of the south-bound lane. The truck was mud-splattered; the side windows were nearly opaque with smeared mud.

He opened the passenger door and was greeted by a large, friendly dog wagging its tail.

"Mully, for crissakes, get in back!"

Shay watched the dog hop between the seats to the space behind and then looked at the driver.

She was a grey-haired woman smoking a cigarette and smiling at him.

"Where you heading?"

"Going west eventually. Avoiding the interstate. In no hurry. Hope to end up in maybe Portland. How far you going?"

He saw that the driver was wearing a light blue work shirt

and faded jeans. She was wearing boots like his and a low-crowned wide-brimmed felt hat. *A cattle rancher*, he thought.

"Throw your gear in the back. I'm heading west a ways, that's for sure."

He put the saddle and his duffel bag in the front of the truck bed and climbed in. The driver started off and shifted through the gears before saying anything.

"Nice looking association saddle you've got there. Saddle-bronc rider, huh?" she said.

"Well, Ma'am," he said, "not really my saddle. Friend gave it to me to sell for him. Tell you the truth, I'm not sure what an association saddle is."

The driver took her eyes off the road and looked at him.

"My name's Irene," she said. "Irene Boyd," she added reaching over to shake hands with a strong grip. "Please don't Ma'am me." Then after a pause added, "An association saddle. That's what you've got there. No horn. Used for saddle bronc riding in the rodeo. Approved by the saddle bronc association, I guess."

He was about to say something, when Mully started licking the back of his neck, almost knocking off his hat.

"Dag nabbit Mully! Quit that! Dog's real friendly. Give her a poke if she's bothering you,"

"No Ma-…, I mean, no problem. Not bothering me," he said, then turned and rubbed the dog's ears. "What kind of a dog is this?"

"Just a mutt, really. Like mulligan stew. Name's Mulligan. Mully for short." She patted the dog on the forehead and added, "What's yours?"

"Lleyellyn Shay. People usually call me Lou Ellen," he said, glancing at her. "I don't mind. Used to it. Easier."

They continued westward at a good clip on the nearly-empty two-lane highway. Both of them were silent for a while.

He looked over his surroundings.

The dashboard was covered with a wild assortment of things. Tools. Documents. Sunglasses. Newspapers. A pair of binoculars. A roll of toilet paper. Magazines. A box of cartridges. A coil of wire. A CB radio was suspended from the ceiling and there was a cell phone plugged into the lighter. Turning back to pet Mully again, he noticed two gun cases leaning in the rear corner of the cab on the driver's side.

Irene broke the silence. "Portland, huh?"

"Well, I'm thinking about heading there. Maybe find a job or something."

"That's a pretty far piece. I'm going southwest as far as the turnoff to my place. Eighty seven miles from Miles City. I can drop you off there. There's not much between here and there, though. Can't say how long it would take to get another ride."

"That's all right, Miss Irene..." he started.

"Just Irene. No Miss. No Ma'am. Irene. Okay?"

"Okay. Irene. You can drop me off anywhere. I can keep hitching. Someone will stop."

The cell phone beeped, and Mully surged forward as though on point.

"Mully, it's for me," Irene told the dog. "Irene here," she said into the phone and then listened.

"Just left Miles City. I'm about two hours out," she said and then listened some more. "Hold off until I'm back. Maybe I can do something," she added and then hung up.

She looked over at Lleyellen.

"There's always something, isn't there?" she said, and then turned her gaze back toward the road.

"Anybody tell you you shouldn't pick up hitchhikers?" he finally said, mostly to break the silence.

Irene seemed to think this over, then looked at him again.

"If you can't trust a cowboy, who can you trust?" she said

and smiled, grin lines prominent on her cheeks and temples.

For some reason, Lleyellyn felt the urge to add, "Well, Irene, I'm not really a cowboy. I just helped out a guy at the rodeo. An ex-rodeo star gave me this buckle and I bought this hat and the boots in town on sale. Don't know nothing about horses or cows, really."

Irene considered this silently, then seemed to concentrate her attention ahead, her eyes squinting. She picked up the microphone for her CB radio and spoke: "Jimbo boy, is that you north bound?"

"Irene. Where are you? Is that you coming toward me with that new trailer?" came the tinny reply over the CB.

"That's me. Say, how's the new baby. You and Beverly better come by the place some weekend soon," Irene said. "You copy?"

"We're coming. Bev's got something she wants to show you. We'll be sure and show up there by dinner time. Call you first. I can see you now. Keep that rig in your lane, now. You hear?"

A speeding cattle truck was fast approaching. Irene gave a wave and the driver honked a loud dopplering reply.

"Looking good there, Jimbo. Where you heading?" Irene again spoke into the CB.

"Lazy R. Load of calves. Then to Billings. See you this Sunday, or the next."

Irene hung up the microphone and checked her rear-view mirror.

"Jimbo's a real nice young man. Been married about a year. I've worked with his wife."

Lleyellen looked at her. Before he could ask the question that was on his mind, she answered it.

"I wear two hats around here," she said. "I have the cattle outfit. And then I'm also a rape crisis counselor for the county. Went to college for social work and that's what I do when I'm needed. Luckily, there's not as many sexual assaults in these parts as in some others, so I'm only needed once in a while. On-call basis," she explained.

Then she turned her eyes directly on him.

"So tell me," she inquired, "what's your story? I know you aren't from around here."

He looked over at her, then turned back to the road.

"You sure you want to hear this? It's kind of a long story," he said.

"We've got a long way to go. I'm all ears if you'd care to talk," Irene said.

Mully leaned forward and gave Irene's cheek a lick and then laid down behind Lleyellyn's seat.

He ran the events of the last few days through his mind. Then he looked up.

"I'm really running away from home, I guess. My mother did know I was leaving, and why. My stepfather was a mean son-of-a-, excuse me, a real s. o. b., and I just had to get away."

He looked over at Irene, who seemed intent on the road, before she glanced over and flashed a brief, encouraging smile.

He wasn't sure why he did it, but for some reason he started telling Irene about his background.

He told her that Mal, his stepfather, hadn't seemed like such a bad guy when he and his mother got married. Mal had a daughter two years older than Lleyellyn. He and his step-sister got along very well.

First Mal started getting abusive to his daughter, Shelly. The county placed her in temporary foster care. Then she just took off.

He supposed it was an aftermath of Mal's time in the war that was the root cause of his problems. He had been a green beret and had seen combat that he rarely talked about. Mal liked to hang around with other vets, drink, smoke pot. Worked seasonally loading barges on the Mississippi.

"My sister sent me a postcard last year. Post marked Carbondale, Illinois. She wrote 'LL, I'm O. K.' and signed it 'Love, S.'"

Lleyellyn told Irene after Shelly left, Mal started taking most of his anger out on Lleyellyn, calling him names and knocking him around.

"He took my dog with him in his truck one time. He probably shot it. The collar was hanging from the rearview mirror in his truck. It looked like it had dried blood on it."

He told her his mother tried to protect him the best she could. His school work suffered. A counselor at the high school helped get him enrolled in the Altennative School where he completed all graduation requirements early. He got his diploma three weeks before the end of the school year.

"I could have gone to the graduation ceremony with the regular high school students, but I decided to get out of town early, away from Mal. Mal was getting worse and it was getting scary. My mother urged me to go.

"I didn't have any money, so I cut down some copper wire off the old telegraph poles along the railroad, and sold it for scrap. Copper's worth a lot right now. I got enough to get an Amtrak ticket to Portland. I guess taking the wire was stealing, but those poles seemed pretty much abandoned to me."

He looked toward Irene. She didn't say anything but he could tell she had been listening to him. She seemed to be very interested, easy to talk to.

"Well, on the train I met a guy about my age. Saddle bronc rider. Name's Tole Winters. Tole was going to his first professional rodeo. He asked me to get off in Montana with him. Glasgow. We went to Miles City by van. Tole broke his arm after the first go-around and was disqualified after the second ... but he was robbed, should of made the finals Sunday. That pretty much soured him on the rodeo."

Irene held out her hand to stop him for a minute.

"I saw the paper the other day. That was Tole on the front page, wasn't it?"

"Yes, Ma-am. Yes, it was."

Irene ignored the Ma'am and didn't correct him this time. He didn't even realize he'd said it.

"From what I remember, you're the bull rider. Am I right?"

He looked at Irene, then, embarrassed, flashed a brief smile and said, "The paper said that. Based on something I said. But no, I'm not a bull rider, or any kind of rider for that matter. I was just helping out my new friend, sort of his agent. Maybe I overdid it a bit when I talked to the reporter."

Irene glanced at him reassuringly, then returned her gaze down the road.

"Well, it was a pretty good article. You must of done your agent job pretty darn good."

They rode on in silence for a while. Irene turned on the radio to check the weather report just before nine o'clock, then pulled over to the side of the road across from a concrete-block building. Lleyellyn thought it might be a cell-phone station or power line transformer or something.

"I gotta take a potty break," Irene said. "Ladies on the left, men on the right," she said, getting out. "Hand me that roll of TP, will you? I'll just be a minute or two."

He got out and walked off into the weeds out of sight. Mully started to follow him at first, until Irene shouted, "Mully! Over here. Girls to the left."

When they got back to the truck, Irene was silent as she let Mully in, fastened her seat-belt and threw the roll of TP on the dash. Then she pulled onto the tarvia and gradually accelerated through the gears.

"You know, Lou Ellen. I've been thinking. Have you called

your mother since you left home?"

"No, but I've only been gone a little while."

"Well, I think you should give her a call. This is your first trip on your own, isn't it?"

He didn't say anything, but took the cell phone when Irene handed it to him.

"I always get good reception along here," she said. "Must be that relay station back there."

He remembered his mother telling him to call his grandmother if he wanted to get in touch. He dialed the six oh eight area code and then his grandmother's familiar number. The phone started ringing almost immediately. On the fourth ring the answering machine came on. He heard his grandmother's recorded message.

"It's me, Gramma. Lleyellyn." He started to say more when Irene held out her hand to stop him.

"Have her call you back on the ranch number," she said and then told him the number. He repeated it to the answering machine, then pressed the end-of-call button.

"She might not reach us on the cell phone much longer. If she calls the ranch, we can get her message on my voice mail anytime."

After a mile or two of silence, Irene said, "I've been thinking it over some. If you want, I can get on the horn and maybe find someone going west who can take you on farther than I can. Maybe there's a trucker I know going your way. I'll give it a try if you want me to."

He didn't say anything before Irene spoke again.

"Since you don't have to be anywhere special at any particular time, maybe you'd like to work for me for a while. Earn a little money. Solidify your plans a little."

"I don't really have any ranch experience," he said.

"If you're willing to work, we'll find something for you to

do. Mr. Montoya, my foreman, can always use some help. The only requirement is a willingness to work and follow directions. If you don't like the job, I'll see that you get back out here on the road and you'll be on your way."

He didn't respond immediately, but it sounded like a real opportunity.

"It could be interesting around the place for the next several weeks," Irene said. "Outfit's leased out to a movie company. Filming a western. Cattle drives and all that. Need help keeping a handle on things."

A few minutes later she added, "Mr. Montoya and I share the cooking duties. You cook?"

Llewellyn laughed.

"I can make only one thing. Learned in eighth grade home economics. Miss Reed taught us how to make a dinner for four in ten minutes or less for less than the cost of a Big Mac, fries and a coke."

Irene wanted to know how it worked out.

"All you need is a couple cans of beans. Kidney. Northern. Navy beans. Doesn't matter. Get the cheapest ones. Add a can of tomato sauce. Then you pick out a ring bologna or maybe a kielbasa. I like linguica best. And an onion."

Irene looked at him. She nodded for him to go on.

"What you do is put the beans in a pot and add the tomato sauce. You chop up the onion. Teacher said to sauté the onions. That means fry 'em in olive oil until browned. Add 'em to the beans. Then you cut up and fry the sausage, too, then add it to the rest. Cook. Slow boil. Simmer, Miss Reed said. About a half hour. No salt needed with canned beans."

"Sounds good to me," Irene said. "Tasty."

"You can bake it, too, if you want. Add a little brown sugar. But I like to add a little jalapeno pepper and cook it on the stove."

"You'll get some chef duty if you work for me. Minnesota

Bean Surprise, how's that sound?" Irene said.

"Well, it's the only thing I ever did that Mal liked. He usually ate most of it."

While he was thinking about Irene's job offer, Irene said, "I'll pay you six bucks an hour plus room and board. The room's in the bunk house. The grub's whatever Mr. Montoya or I decide to fix. Plus your Minnesota bean dish when it's your turn."

"Sounds real interesting." Then, after briefly considering her offer, he said, " I'd like to give the job a try."

oOo

As they continued southwesterly there was nothing except pasture, grassland and freshly planted land as far as they could see. He did see an occasional hawk atop a telephone pole and twice pheasants flew across their path, one coming so close he ducked.

Finally, Irene spoke up.

"Last chance, we're almost at the turnoff to my outfit. It's not too late to get out, if you've changed your mind."

"No. I'm kinda looking forward to the job. And the homecooking."

oOo

The turn-off came up suddenly. A faded sign leaned into the wind. It read *BOYD RANCH – REGISTERED HEREFORDS.* Irene slowed and smoothly negotiated the turn. Pavement quickly gave way to gravel, but Irene maintained her speed.

"Still a ways to go," she said. "About forty mile."

Irene tried the CB but got no response. Then she picked up the cell phone and quickly keyed the number.

"Damn thing's out of range. Practically useless out here. Should be there in forty-five minutes, or so."

As they drove, Irene gestured to the passing land.

"Good grass this spring, so far. Better than usual rain."

As they topped a small rise, she said, "This was prime buffalo land a hundred and forty years ago. That little stream ahead is Buffalo Creek. I found a Buffalo skull when I was fishing there once, when I was a kid." Then she looked at him and said, "It is pretty darned good cattle country, too. When it rains enough."

He watched the scenery roll by. It hadn't changed much at all since they left Miles City. In the distance he saw the dust of an approaching vehicle of some kind. Irene pulled over onto the grass shoulder to allow plenty of room. Finally they could tell it was a car. From the top-mounted lights, he thought it must be a deputy sheriff or some kind of patrol car.

"Warden Jimmy," Irene announced as the approaching car slowed and stopped along-side Irene.

Irene let the dust cloud dissipate, then rolled down her window.

"Morning, Jimmy. Where you going in such a hurry?"

"Irene, how's it going?" the warden said. "I see you got yourself a new trailer."

"It was time, don't you think?" she said. "What brings you out this way?"

"Just routine patrol. Stopped by Cat-tail Lake and the other spots and stuff. I haven't seen hardly anybody all morning."

"Well, say hello to the Missus. You better get back to work. Tough to make your quota out in the middle of nowhere, ain't it?" she asked, teasingly, trying to get a rise from the game warden.

The warden gave her a brief smile and didn't reply. Then he pulled slowly forward, keeping the dust to a minimum until he was of range.

"Being a game warden out here can be pretty lonely. He's got an area about the size of some states. Gets busy during hunting season, though."

"What kind of things do they hunt out here?"

Irene gestured with her hand to both sides of the road.

"Lots of antelope. Mule deer. Winter time, coyote hunting is a big sport. Then you've got your pheasants. Quail. Fishing's not too bad either. Some of these streams look pretty tiny. There's good sized trout in the deeper bends. Sportsman's paradise, they say."

They gradually approached a willow-lined stream. A sign said *NARROW BRIDGE*. Irene eased the truck to a stop on the bridge. Then she rummaged around on the dashboard and picked up a small metal box.

"Lou Ellen, since we've just confirmed there's no game warden around, what say we take a minute or two and test the recreational potential of Buffalo Creek."

Mully jumped out of the cab behind Irene. He followed them along the bank on the downstream side of the bridge. Irene pulled a folding knife out of a pocket and cut off two straight willow shoots. Then she deftly cut off the side branches and handed one to Lleyellyn.

"Here's your pole," she said, before opening the metal box and removing two coiled lengths of fishing line with lures attached.

"Tie this to your pole," she said as she handed one coil to him. "These lures are called Super-Dupers. Been around for decades. My dad used them. Little more rugged than a spinner and don't get snagged as easily."

"Mully! Stay here!" she commanded the dog, which immediately sat down and watched her.

"Trout fish before?" she asked.

He shook his head.

"Okay then, watch me. We don't want to spook the fish."

He followed as Irene carefully tiptoed back to the road keeping away from the stream bank.

Irene was amazingly agile for her age and size. Together they crept across the bridge to the far edge of the stream, slowly placed their lures over the edge of the bank and lowered them into the dark pool under the bridge.

oOo

His lure broke beneath the surface and he could see it sparkling in the current. Within seconds something grabbed it and he yanked the pole up and the hooked fish flashed over his head and landed behind him in the grass.

"Didn't play that one much, did you," Irene said with a chuckle.

He bent down to pick up the wiggling trout. The fish squirmed out of his hand before he could get a firm hold of it. Irene stepped over, took the fish, broke its neck, and removed the hook.

"My dad taught me that trick to put the fish quickly out of its misery. I don't like to see any critter suffer any more than they have to."

She held up the trout.

"Ten, maybe eleven inches. Perfect eating size. Good fishing."

They fished that first pool and two others downstream. When they had six trout, Irene said they had enough for breakfast and they returned to the truck.

oOo

"Almost there," Irene announced as she slowed to cross on a narrow one-lane culvert.

He didn't see any buildings until they topped a small rise. Ahead was a grove of trees, a white porch was visible, set back some fifty yards from the road.

Irene pulled slowly up to a mail box.

"Check the mail, will you, hon?" she said.

He opened a super-sized rusted metal box with peeling letters *OYD RA CH* on the side. He pulled out an accumulation of mail, letters, magazines and a small package. Irene glanced at the stack of mail.

"Just put it here on the console," she said, before pulling into the driveway and proceeding toward the house.

The white porch decorated a two-story, four-square white wood-sided house. Across the driveway and slightly to the rear were several out-buildings painted dark red. The grass had been recently mowed, the yard kept neat, the buildings freshly painted.

As they pulled up to the porch, Mully crawled out from behind the seats, knocked the mail off the console and climbed over Lleyellyn, eager to get out. He opened the door and the dog leaped out and ran toward one of the red painted buildings.

"Dog's looking for Mr. Montoya," Irene said. "Really his dog. Found her along our road. Somebody dumped her."

He watched as Mully ran toward the building.

"That's the bunk house," Irene said as the door opened and a small man wearing khaki from head to toe stepped out and bent down and petted the dog prancing around in front of him, tail seriously awag.

"That's Mr. Montoya," Irene said. "Come along. I'll introduce you."

They both climbed out of the truck and started toward the

bunk house. Montoya saw them coming and headed their way, Mully stopping on the bunk house porch to take a drink from a water dish.

"Mr. Montoya," Irene said by way of introduction, "this here's Lleyellyn Shay. He's willing to give us a hand for a while."

Montoya reached out and they shook hands.

"Hey, Lleyellyn," he said. "Welcome."

Montoya, he observed, was short, perhaps five-foot six, dark complexion and with a pencil-thin mustache and piercing, near-black eyes. He gave an economical smile. His handshake was firm.

After glancing at Irene, Montoya turned back and said, "We'll find something for you to do."

Then, giving Irene his full attention, he added, "Problem's solved. Truck'll be here tomorrow. The bank called and said the check cleared this afternoon."

Irene didn't say anything to this, but after a pause, she changed the subject.

"Mr. Montoya, show Lleyellyn the bunk house and where to put his stuff." Then almost as an afterthought she added, "Dinner about ready?"

"Almost," Montoya said. "Be ready about six."

"I'll clean these fish we just caught first. We can have 'em in the morning for breakfast," Irene said.

Montoya offered to help Shay with his gear, but he said he could manage okay. He followed Montoya, carrying his duffel bag and Tole's saddle. He glimpsed Mully flash by chasing a rabbit.

Mr. Montoya held the door open for him. Inside, eight or ten bunk beds were arranged in two rows in the main room. Rolled up mattresses were neatly aligned on each bunk. There were green foot lockers at the end of each bed.

"This is the bunk room. No one's here this time of year, so

take any one you want. Put your stuff down, and I'll show you around."

Lleyellyn placed his duffel bag on a bed next to a window and put the saddle on the floor.

"You saw the lavatory as you came in," Montoya said, gesturing toward a door they had passed.

"On this end, my room's on the left and the storage room on the right. You can put your saddle in there. Usually keep this room locked up."

He picked up the saddle and carried it toward the storage room. Montoya unlocked the door with a key he removed from a pants pocket. The room was orderly with shelves along the back wall.

"Set the saddle here," Montoya said, pointing to the corner with a tip of his hat. "Take what bed linen and towels you need from over there."

He selected sheets, a blanket, a pillow and other linen, then carried them out to the main room.

"When you get done making up your bed come on into the house. We'll be eating pretty soon. Use the back door. Hang your hat on the back porch," Montoya said. "Irene doesn't like us wearing our hats at the dinner table."

He made up the bunk he had picked out and emptied his gear into a foot locker together with his folded-up duffel bag.

With time to spare, he went to the lavatory. It was a surprisingly big room with two toilet stalls, two urinals, several sinks and a large communal shower. It was spotlessly clean.

After washing up and running a comb through his hair, Lleyellyn walked across the yard to the main house. Mully greeted him when he opened the back screen door. He placed his hat on the rack next to a tan Stetson he recognized as Montoya's.

He hesitated before opening the closed glass door to the main house, wondering if he should knock. Before he made up his mind, Irene opened the door.

"Don't be bashful," she said. "Come on in."

It was an immense kitchen. A big black cook stove dominated one wall. The long oak table was set with three place settings. He was surprised to see Montoya at the stove wearing a blue apron.

"Mr. Montoya's making one of his specialties," Irene said. "Do you like chicken?"

"Sure," he said. The smell of garlic and oregano filled the room. "Sure smells good." He thought Montoya was fixing some Mexican specialty when Irene spoke up.

"Chicken cacciatore. One of my favorites. I know it has to take a while longer to simmer. Go in the living room. Want a soda, iced tea or something?"

"Mountain Dew would be great, if you have it," he said. "But if not, iced tea will do."

As he followed Irene into the living room, Mully started barking from the front porch. Irene parted the curtains and said, "There's a sheriff's car coming up the drive. Wonder what he wants."

She motioned for Shay to take a seat and stepped out onto the porch.

"Quiet down, Mully!" Lleyellyn heard her say and recognized the crunch of gravel as a squad car pulled behind Irene's new trailer.

He heard Irene greet the deputy, but couldn't hear what they were saying after she closed the door.

He had taken a few sips of his drink when Irene stuck her head in.

"Lleyellyn. Deputy Thompson wants to talk to you. Can you come out here?"

Puzzled, he set his drink down on a magazine sitting on a side table and walked out onto the porch.

The deputy was standing next to his car.

"Lleyellyn Shay?" he inquired.

"Yes, sir. That's me."

"I need to talk to you. Would you mind sitting in the front seat with me so we can talk in private?"

He watched Irene go back in the house. He stepped off the porch and walked behind the deputy's car and sat in the front seat.

"Let me turn these radios off so we won't be interrupted," the deputy said, turning several dials. "I'm Deputy Bob Thompson, Lleyellyn."

They shook hands.

"This is difficult. I've been asked to tell you that your mother is dead. I'm so very sorry."

Lleyellyn was stunned. He sat there looking into the deputy's steady gaze, not quite sure if he had heard right. He started to ask a question, then looked away. Finally, he managed to say,

"How...?"

"I've been told she was stabbed to death," the deputy said.

"It was Mal, wasn't it?" Lleyellyn blurted out.

"I don't know the details, son. Here is what I was told," he said, glancing at typed notes, perhaps an email.

"Your mother's body was found when she didn't report to work last Friday. May seventeenth. At first they were looking for her husband... is that Mal? And you. They found out you had taken the train and they had an officer waiting in Portland. When you didn't get off there, they weren't sure where you were. In the meantime, investigators concluded that Mal was the killer. He's on the run and they're looking for him. You were traced when you called your grandmother today."

He tried to listen to the deputy. Tears welled in his eyes. He couldn't help but think about the last time he had seen his mother and how she had wanted him to get away from Mal.

"That damned Mal," he finally managed. "My mother said she could handle him."

Then he sat there silently sobbing to himself.

The deputy reached over and put his hand on Lleyellyn's arm.

"Lleyellyn, there's two things I want you to do. Call your grandmother. She's waiting for your call. They say she is real concerned for you."

Then handing him a card, he added, "When you finish talking to your grandmother, call the Winona investigator. I've written his name and phone number on the back of my card. He has some questions he'd like answered. He's in charge of the investigation of your mother's death. He said you can call him collect."

Shay took the card and looked at the deputy. Then he blew his nose using a Kleenex the deputy handed him, put the card in a shirt pocket, and opened the door.

"Lleyellyn," the deputy said, "I really am sorry."

He mumbled his thanks, shook the deputy's outstretched hand, and stepped out of the car just as Irene opened the door and came out onto the porch.

"What's ....?" she started, her question left unasked when she realized he was crying.

She hurried down the steps and hugged him tight. She patted his back several times as she looked over his shoulder at the grim-faced deputy.

"Irene, this young man just learned that his mother was murdered," the deputy said, slowly shaking his head. Then he got in his car, backed it up, turned and retreated the way he had come.

oOo

Irene gently persuaded Lleyellyn to come in the house. She sat next to him on the couch and Montoya came in and sat across from them in a rocking chair.

Without prompting, he repeated everything the deputy had told him.

"Oh, honey, we're so sorry," Irene said, while Montoya nodded his head in agreement, a concerned look on his face. He remained silent.

"You best call your grandmother. We'll leave you alone so you can talk privately."

As she got up and went into the kitchen, Montoya got up to follow her, giving Lleyellyn a brief pat on the shoulder. He looked up and gave an appreciative smile at this unexpected small gesture.

"Thanks," he managed to say.

oOo

His grandmother must have been expecting his call. She answered in the middle of the first ring.

Shay had always enjoyed talking to his grandmother. She was one of the only people, besides his mother, that he had been able to count on. When she answered, she just said, "Lou Ellen?"

"Yes, Gramma, it's me. They just told me what happened," he said in a high-pitched voice that sounded strange even to him.

His grandmother remained quiet. He thought she must be crying. Then she told him what she knew. How the cops were looking for him at first, maybe as a suspect. Then they told her they knew it was Mal. His bloody footprints were found in the trailer and near his pickup.

"She told me to get out," Lleyellyn said. "She was afraid of what Mal might do to me. She said she could handle him, take care of herself."

His grandmother remained silent for a moment before speaking.

"She was afraid of him. She was planning to leave just as soon you were away and safe. He probably found out you'd left or that she was about to go herself. I don't know. I should have done something."

He let this sink in. Finally, he asked, "When is the funeral?"

"Hon, she wanted to be cremated. She told me that several times. There was no real funeral. When you are back someday, we can scatter her ashes together if you'd like. In the Mississippi, or maybe Brady's Bluff. They were some of her favorite places."

Lleyellyn told her that he was supposed to call the Winona investigator and that he wondered if he should come home to take care of the ashes now.

"You stay where you are. They told me you've found a place and a job. You come here and no telling what Mal might do. They haven't found him yet and it's nearly a week. Found his truck in the yard, but no sign of him."

While he thought this over, his grandmother added, "Lou Ellen, honey, I've got to tell you this. You'll get arrested if you come back to Minnesota. It's about some copper wire you took from along the tracks. The officer told me they won't come after you outside the state, but if you show up here you'd probably have to spend a day or two in the hoosegow until bail is set."

"Ah, Grams," he said, "that wire wasn't being used. It was abandoned."

"I don't know about that. I'm just letting you in on what the officer told me."

They talked some more and he promised to call again in a day or two.

"You have the number here where I'll be," he said. "Call me if they catch Mal."

oOo

At Irene's urging, Lleyellyn managed to eat some of the Mr. Montoya's chicken dish, but he didn't taste anything. He excused himself, saying, "I'm supposed to call the investigator in Winona."

He went into the living room and fished the card Deputy Thompson had given him from a pocket and called the number written on the back. He was quickly put through.

"Investigator Williams," a voice said.

"I'm Lleyellyn Shay. A deputy here in Montana told me to call you."

The voice on the other end was quiet for a moment. He guessed he was closing his office door, maybe turning on a recording device.

"Yes. Thanks for calling Mr. Shay. First let me say that I'm sorry about your mother. She was a good hard-working lady. I know that."

He waited a few seconds, then said, "Yes she was. She sure was."

"Mr. Shay, I wanted you to call me so I can maybe get some information."

"I hope I can help," he said. "What would you like to know?"

"Did Mal get physical? With you? With your mother?"

He couldn't help but think back to the house and the times he had hidden from Mal. How afraid he had been.

"Well, he beat me up pretty often. I had to lock myself in my room. I left because it wasn't getting any better. My mom told me I should get away. Start fresh. She said she could handle Mal."

"Any idea where he might have gone?" the investigator asked.

"I don't really. I know he used to spend a lot of time in the backwaters. Hunting. Fishing. Camping out. I think he sort of lived on the river when he got out of the army, but I don't know where. He never took me with him fishing or anything."

"Mr. Shay, I don't have many questions right now. We know it was Mal that did it. We are looking for him now. Some things might come up. How can I reach you?"

Lleyellyn was thinking where Mal might be hiding, when he remembered something.

"Mal did have a boat. It was always in our yard. Flat-bottomed. Aluminum. Kinda cammo-looking. He painted it. It was always behind the house. I noticed it was gone a week or so before I left. I don't know if he was using it or if he sold it, or what."

"I'll check into it," the investigator said. "How can I get a hold of you?"

"You can get me here where I'm working" he said, before giving the investigator Irene's phone number at the Boyd Ranch. Then before hanging up, he added, "Will you call me if you catch Mal?"

"Happy to," the investigator said. "We've got a lot of people looking for him. We'll find him."

oOo

After finishing the call, he went into the kitchen and told Irene and Mr. Montoya he was going to try and get some rest. It was early, but he felt drained and tired. They tried again but couldn't get him to take another bite.

"Hon, if there is anyone else you want to call, go ahead. Use the phone in the office so you'll have some privacy," Irene said.

The only person he could call a friend was Tole, but he didn't know if he should bother him with a call or not. Tole was his friend. His only friend.

He assumed it was the uncle who answered.

"Can I talk to Tole?" he said. "It's Lleyellyn Shay from Montana."

"Hey! Bud, how you doing?" Tole said by way of greeting.

He hesitated a few moments, then said, "That goddamned stepfather of mine killed my mother. They just got hold of me a few minutes ago to tell me."

There was a long pause. He heard the line crackle.

"Shit man, that's tough..... Real sorry to hear that...... How you doing?"

"Still numb. Fucker's loose. They're looking. But haven't caught him yet."

"Where are you?" Tole said.

Lleyellyn told him about getting picked up by Irene and being hired to work at her ranch and about the motion picture that was going to be filmed there.

"You coming back here?"

"There's no funeral planned. My gramma says we can hold a memorial later," Lleyellyn said, then added, "She told me there's a warrant for me in Minnesota for stealing copper. If I come back, I'll be arrested."

There was a pause, before Tole spoke. "If I can do anything for you, just let me know. Okay?"

Lleyellyn thanked his friend, asked about his injured shoulder, and said he would let him know if he found out anything.

Before hanging up, he said, "One more thing, I plan to put a sign up about your saddle to try and sell it to someone with the movie crowd."

oOo

Lleyellyn went out to the bunkhouse. He took a quick shower, slipped on a pair of shorts, turned out the lights and went to bed. He couldn't sleep. Thoughts of his mother, Mal's meanness, the life they had lived after his mother remarried, and similar things raced through his mind so crowded together that it kept him awake. He tried to will himself to sleep, but couldn't. Finally he got up, put on his shirt and pants and went out and sat on the porch. The wind had died down. It was quiet, the silence interrupted only by the rhythmic squeaking of the windmill. Mully came from out of the darkness and sat down next to him.

Shay heard the back door slam and stopped petting the dog as Mully stood up. Then he saw that it was Montoya walking toward the bunk house. Montoya didn't say anything, but he came and sat down next to Lleyellyn.

Then he said, "It's tough, kid. Losing a parent is hard. Losing your mother like that is bad. The loss of a loved one is about the most difficult thing there is. Anytime you want to talk about it, let me know."

Montoya had surprised him. He wasn't sure what to say. He didn't know how Montoya could help. He sat silently. Finally Montoya stood up and put his hand on his shoulder.

"Just ask," he said. "I'm going to hit the hay."

The dog and Lleyellyn stayed on the porch a while longer. The outside light by the barn was not very bright. The light in the kitchen was turned off. Irene had gone to bed. More stars than he had ever seen filled the sky. There wasn't another light visible anywhere.

He heard the door open. Montoya came and sat down next to him.

"I don't know what Irene told you about me. Why I was sent away to prison."

"Irene never said anything to me. Just that you were her foreman."

Montoya told Lleyellyn his history. He had grown up on a big cattle ranch north of Miles City. His father was the foreman and his grandfather had held the same job before him.

Montoya's father married his high school sweetheart. She was an O'Brien. They had three children. The two daughters had fair complexions like their mother.

The owner's only son was two years ahead of Montoya in school. They didn't pal around, but never had any issues. They each had their own circle of friends.

Montoya spent his summers working as a cowboy on the ranch and was an accomplished horseman and indispensable during the spring roundups.

"The owner's son raped Irene when I was a sophomore. They were both seniors. At his trial he got three of his buddies to testify that they were all on a hunting trip in Wyoming when the assault occurred."

Montoya explained that the attacker was found not guilty although not everyone was convinced.

"I knew all three of his alibi witnesses were lying when they all started driving new Silverado pickups a week or two after the trial. Putting sugar in their gas tanks didn't seem like enough."

Montoya paused and Lleyellyn kneaded Mully's neck.

"I heard the shit head and his three pals laughing about the trial at a party before he left for college in Sioux Falls. I followed the fucker there. Used some of my ranch skills. Castrated the bastard. Then I dropped him off at the E. R.

"Most everyone knew there should have been a guilty verdict. Even though I was arrested the next day, my father got to keep his foreman job. Stayed on at the ranch even after he retired. Died there when I was in prison. The boss knew his son was guilty."

Lleyellyn wasn't sure if Montoya wanted a response.

"Looking back, I don't see how I could have done anything different," Montoya said. "Justice had not been done."

Lleyellyn could see the reasoning behind what Montoya had told him, but taking the law into his own hands was something he had never considered.

"It's not right, your stepdad getting away with murder. We should do something."

"You mean, like, maybe track him down for the sheriff?" Lleyellyn said.

"Something like that. I can tell you one thing for sure, I have no plans to go back to prison."

CHAPTER NINE

May 22

It was well after midnight when he finally went in and got into bed. His thoughts flared up again but somehow he fell asleep. When he woke up it was just starting to get light. He heard the shower going and then a few minutes later Montoya stepped out of the bathroom followed by a cloud of steam. He was dressed in clean-crisp khakis. He was putting on his tan Stetson when he noticed that Lleyellyn was awake.

"Morning. Breakfast in about twenty minutes. See you over at the house."

As soon as Lleyellyn entered the kitchen he knew that Irene and Montoya were sizing him up to see how he was getting along.

"Morning," Irene said. "Sit down. Breakfast will be ready in a few minutes."

He sat down across from Montoya who raised the coffee pot in greeting, gesturing toward a mug in front of Lleyellyn.

"No thanks," he said. "Could I have a Mountain Dew?"

"Help yourself," Irene said. "Look in the refrigerator. On the door."

He took the soft drink, popped the can and sat down again.

"Manage any sleep?" Irene asked.

He took a sip of his drink, glanced at Montoya, then flashed a small smile toward Irene.

"Not much. Maybe a little," he said. "But I'm feeling a little better."

Irene put two pan fried trout on each plate, placed one in front of Montoya, then one in front of Lleyellyn. She carried a plate to her place at the table and sat down. She passed around a platter of bacon, scrambled eggs and biscuits. He didn't feel particularly hungry. He cut a biscuit in half, made a bacon sandwich and suddenly realized that he needed something to eat. Irene and Montoya watched him eat his breakfast without saying anything at all. When he had finished and his plate was empty, Irene said, "There's seconds."

Lleyellyn looked up, then back at his plate.

"I didn't realize I was hungry. I've never had fish for breakfast before. It was all really good, but I've had plenty. Thanks."

He stood up, picked up his plate and utensils and carried them over to the sink.

"Son, let that wait," Irene said. "Sit down. We've got some work for you today."

After he returned to the table and sat down, Irene continued.

"You got some tough news yesterday. I'm sure it must be hard to keep from thinking about the tragedy. Everybody's different, but I've learned a few things in my time. Keeping busy. Physically. That's what helps the most."

He looked at Irene. She reached out and took his hand.

"Lleyellyn, we want to help you if we can. Today I've got some chores lined up for you that will keep you busy. This evening we'll talk some. I'd like to know more about your mother. I'm sure she was a nice person."

He looked at Irene. He could see real concern in her eyes. He glanced over at Montoya who was studying him intently.

"She's right," he said, "Irene's pretty good about things like this."

Lleyellyn looked from one to the other.

"You've both been good to me." Then looking at Montoya, he asked, "What jobs have you got?"

"I'm the one with the jobs today," Irene said. "First I need you to straighten up the storage shed. Then I want you to empty the trailer. It is pretty full of feed supplements and other supplies. Need to rotate the stock. Put the newest dated stuff on the bottom and the older stuff on the top. Take your time. Do it right. Mr. Montoya will show you where things go."

"Okay. I can do that," he said. "Anything else?"

"Well, yes. When you finish up in the storage shed, I'd like you to check the fences."

He didn't say anything, but his look must have told Irene he needed more of an explanation.

"What you do is ride around the entire perimeter of the place. Take a notebook. Mark down any parts of the fence that need mending. Barbed wire. Posts. Braces. Anything that needs fixing. Write it down. Kinda make your own diagram so you know where the problems are. We'll have you make the repairs tomorrow or the next day."

He listened to her instructions. Before he could ask about the work, Montoya added, "There's a little over twenty miles of perimeter fence. We'll have you check it out by Jeep. Ever drive a stick-shift?"

"Well, no. I don't have a driver's license," Shay said. "Never had a car."

"Mr. Montoya will show you how to drive the Jeep. You won't need a license. It's all private land. You won't be driving on any public roads."

Lleyellyn helped Irene put the rest of the dishes in the sink and then followed Montoya outside.

"Ready to get started?" Montoya asked.

"You bet."

"The supply shed's back there," Montoya said, nodding his hat brim to the far side of the bunk house. He fell in beside Montoya as they walked along the drive to where Irene's pickup and trailer were parked beside a neat, red building. As they walked, Mully sidled up to Montoya.

"Where you been, girl?" Montoya said, giving the dog's ears a rub.

Montoya stepped up to the door and pulled a key from his pocket. Shay noted that the door was reinforced, the lock sturdy.

"We keep this locked. Pretty valuable stuff in here. Veterinary medicines. Chemicals."

The building seemed bigger than it had looked from the outside. Shelves along one wall were filled with neatly labeled bottles, cartons and other containers. There were several piles of big brightly colored plastic sacks arranged along the opposite wall and along the sides.

"I want you to dust the stuff on the shelves. The sacks should be moved outside and then the floor swept. When you get done with that, move in the sacks from the trailer and stack them neatly. The stuff in here, you can stack on top of the new pile. We want to use up the oldest stuff first. Any questions?"

"Not really. Where's the brooms and stuff?"

"Everything you need is in that cabinet over there," Montoya said. "When you finish up here, I'll introduce you to the Jeep."

Lleyellyn spent almost until lunch time getting the supply shed cleaned up and the supplies neatly stacked. He was surprised when he checked his watch. The time had gone by faster than he had expected. The physical labor had helped take his mind off his mother's murder.

Before going to the house to get lunch, he hurried to the bunkhouse, quickly showered, and put on a fresh pair of jeans and a clean shirt.

He entered the house by the back door. The kitchen was empty. A note on the table told him to help himself. Sandwiches were in the refrigerator. He poured a glass of milk, took a bite of an egg salad sandwich and picked up the note. On the second page, Irene had written, *"Lleyellyn, start checking the perimeter fence after lunch. The Jeep is in the machine shed. Tank's full. Key is in it. Use this tablet and diagram what you see. Mark the areas that need fixing. We'll see you at suppertime. Irene."*

He was surprised to find that he was still hungry. He ate a second sandwich, put the dish and empty glass in the sink, grabbed a Mountain Dew out of the refrigerator and headed out to the barn.

Hope I can figure out how to drive a stick. The only time he had ever driven was when his mother let him try out her old Honda Civic in the high school parking lot. It was an automatic.

He walked from the bright sunlight into the darkness of the barn. Dust particles hung suspended in shafts of sunlight that traced their way up to several small holes in the ceiling. When his sight adjusted to the shadows, he was surprised to see the Jeep. It looked old with a small windshield and no top. From its drab color it was obviously military surplus.

A key was in the ignition mounted on the dash. He climbed in and sat behind the wheel and put both hands on the steering wheel. He tried out the pedals. He knew what the throttle was. He knew there was a brake. He wasn't too sure about the other pedal. He put his right hand on the gear shift lever that protruded from the floor. He moved the lever and looked at the diagram etched in the plastic knob. Then he turned the ignition key. The vehicle leaped a few feet forward and the engine died. He was glad no one was around.

He checked the glove compartment and found a faded dog-eared army operator's manual. He took it out in the sunlight so he could read it better. There was a page of simple instructions about starting and driving. He followed the instructions, depressed the clutch, shifted into neutral and turned the key again. The engine came to life. He put his foot on the brake pedal and released the emergency brake. Then he shifted the knob into first, and slowly lifted up on the clutch pedal. The engine started to sputter, but smoothed out as he applied pressure to the throttle and the Jeep slowly moved forward out the door and into the sunlight. He hit the brake and the engine died. He was smiling as he started it again, and then moved forward again. He slowly circled the barn for practice, stopping and starting several times. He headed down the driveway toward the road and shifted into second, then turned around and returned to the yard.

Lleyellyn set the emergency brake and ran into the house to get the notebook he had left on the table, and another Mountain Dew. He checked the kitchen clock and wrote "Left by Jeep at 12:47. Lleyellyn" on the bottom of Irene's note.

He was actually looking forward to checking the fence. As he climbed into the Jeep he was surprised to see Mully run out from under the well house and jump into the seat next to him. Mully looked at him. The dog loved riding in the car.

"You sure about this, Mully?"

The Jeep was surprisingly simple to handle. There was a two-tracked trail along the fence line and it was easy to follow it and keep an eye on the fence. He drove in first gear, no more than ten or twelve miles an hour. He noted the mileage on the odometer and wrote it down in the notebook. 187,897.3 It would help him locate places that needed fixing.

Shay watched the fence carefully. Every post was straight. The wires taunt. The trail was mostly level but there were small depressions and some rocks. When the track started up a small rise Lleyellyn had to skirt a rock outcropping, but he had no trouble handling the Jeep. The outcropping was the end of a hogback that led away to the south. Where the fence crossed the rocky area he noted the first fence damage. He stopped, carefully set the emergency brake and turned off the motor. Mully actually led the way over to the fence. The post was sheared off just above a flat, rocky area. The fence was leaning, the two lower strands pulled free of the staples that were bent nearly straight.

Mully was sniffing the post. Lleyellyn saw tufts of brown fur on one of the barbs. He took a closer look, but had no idea what had happened. He thought he might be able to make a temporary repair but there were no tools in the Jeep. He drew a diagram in Irene's notebook. He made a notation about the broken post at the rocky outcropping and then checked the odometer. He had driven 3.4 miles. He wrote that down. It would be easy to relocate the exact spot.

From the top of the incline he could see ahead to where a willow-lined arroyo crossed the track, then the track curved away from the fence to avoid a steep bank.

He and Mully got out of the Jeep and followed the nearly dry stream to the fence line. The water wasn't flowing but there were several pools. Lleyellyn observed tracks in the mud. Deer. Raccoon. Others he didn't recognize.

The fence was hidden in the brush. He walked the fence in both directions. It seemed to be sound. No broken wires. The posts solid. He thought it would be best to cut back the brush along the fence. He made a note in the book. 4.6 miles, he calculated.

He lost Mully for a few minutes while she chased a jackrabbit along the fence. The dog returned, took a drink from one of the pools and then beat him back to the Jeep.

Lleyellyn stopped the Jeep and looked blankly ahead.

Did my leaving home cause my mother's death? Mal had been mean, but his mother seemed to be able to keep him at bay. He didn't remember Mal ever hitting her, but he had make threats.

Then he thought about his mother being stabbed. The suffering. And Mal getting away. He couldn't help it. He started crying silently to himself.

Then he stepped down and slapped the hood of the Jeep.

"Damn. Damn. Damn, that Mal!" he shouted.

He looked up and saw Mully still sitting in the passenger seat. She was looking at him, her head at an inquiring tilt.

"Okay, Mully, let's go."

They drove west along the fence. The odometer showed they had gone another mile and a half when ahead he saw the vast sprawl of a prairie dog town. Mully hopped out and ran toward one animal that quickly retreated out of sight down a burrow. The dog must have played the game before. She returned to the Jeep, hopped in and ignored the prairie dogs popping up out of range across several acres.

Signs of the prairie dog colony spread out across the fence line. He drove to the westerly boundary of the ranch, stopped. He got out to see if the tunnels had loosened any fence posts. He found one that wiggled a little, but the wire strands were tight and intact. Then he turned north along the edge of the property.

So far he hadn't seen any cattle. The grass was long and appeared ungrazed.

Atop a small rise he looked off to a small man-made pond behind a grass-covered earthen dam. There were cattle tracks in the mud, but no cattle. As he drove closer, a great blue heron straightened up near the edge of the pond bank and flew off.

The small draw below the dam crossed the fence line. As he approached he could see that the fence was down. Lleyellyn got out of the Jeep and followed the draw to the fence. Two posts were down, obviously pulled from the ground. Lleyellyn guessed the posts had come loose following a heavy rain. He didn't see any sign of the old post holes which had silted in.

He went back and looked in the Jeep. The only tool he could

find was a short entrenching tool and an ax. He scouted around in the draw until he found a sapling that would act as a support. He cut down the tree and removed the side branches leaving a five foot long trunk with a short fork at the end. With the entrenching tool he managed to dig a hole between the two downed posts. He placed the fork under the top strand of wire and struggled to put the other end in the hole he had dug. The fence stood upright. It probably wouldn't stand another downpour but it might last until permanent repairs could be made.

When he got back to the Jeep, the dog wasn't in sight. He threw the tools in the back and started the motor. Mully came out of the brush and jumped in the passenger seat. She had been exploring.

After carefully marking the spot on his diagram, he put the vehicle in gear and continued following along the fence line. As they topped the next rise he surprised a pair of coyotes trotting along together in the twin tracks of the trail. The coyotes stopped and looked back at the approaching Jeep, then veered off to the east and up another small rise. The bigger of the two stopped and looked back again, then joined its companion and topped the rise. Two pair of ears bounced up into sight repeatedly as they continued trotting away just over the crest of the hill. Mully watched the coyotes intently, but made no move to give chase. When the ears were finally fully out of sight, she barked loudly. He glanced over.

"Good job, Mully! You scared them off."

They came to the end of the western stretch of the fence and turned east. He still hadn't seen any cattle. Ahead was a windmill. A corrugated steel stock tank beside the windmill appeared to be full. As they approached he saw that the tank was over-flowing. A covey of grouse flew away and the dog jumped out and gave half-hearted chase. Mully veered off and stopped below the tank where a stream meandered off toward a cottonwood tree. The dog was drinking as he pulled to a stop in the shade of the tree.

"Time to eat, Mully."

Lleyellyn took a plastic bag out of the cooler and fished out a Mountain Dew. As he unwrapped a sandwich the dog came over and he tossed her half of a bologna sandwich. Mully gulped it down and sat, eyes fixed on him, waiting for seconds.

Shay looked at his watch. He'd been riding the fence line for a little over three hours and he estimated he was a little over half done. He ignored the dog while he ate his half of the sandwich, then unwrapped another.

"Like cheese?" he asked Mully.

The dog wagged her tail. He tore off a piece of his second sandwich and tossed it to the dog.

"Eat slower," he said.

Lleyellyn took his time finishing his half of the cheese sandwich, then gave a corner to Mully who made quick work of it. He downed the rest of his soda and threw the can and wrappers in the back of the Jeep. He walked over to the tank to wash his hands. The water was clear and biting cold. He removed his hat and dunked his head underwater, than brushed his hair straight back with his hands. Mully came over and put her front paws on the edge of the tank and tried to take another drink. The dog was panting and looked hot. He gave Mully a boost and the dog edged into the water and swam across the tank and back. He helped the dog out and was rewarded with a shower when Mully shook herself, then ran back and jumped in the Jeep.

The only thing he noticed as he followed the fence to the east was a corral and loading chute in the corner where the fence line met the eastern boundary. There were weeds growing inside the corral. It hadn't been used for a while.

As they turned to follow the fence back to the house, he realized that the track he was following paralleled the road. He hadn't noticed until a cattle truck came toward him raising a cloud of dust and sounded a long note with its horn. He kept an eye on the fence and a lookout for more traffic. Two other cattle trucks and a pickup passed. Everyone honked or waved.

Finally, he could see the buildings ahead. He was almost back to the house. He didn't see any problems with the fence on the easterly side along the road.

Irene and Montoya probably check it every time they drive past.

He heard another horn sound when he was about an eighth of a mile from the house. He looked over to see Irene's familiar blue pickup on the road. Mully stood up and barked at the pickup. Irene waved from the driver's seat. She was alone. Mully had recognized her immediately. The dog jumped down and raced for the house, going faster than the Jeep.

oOo

Irene was standing behind her truck petting Mully when Lleyellyn drove into the yard. He gave her a wave then parked the Jeep in the machine shed. As he walked toward Irene, she shouted over to him, "Come over to the kitchen when you get cleaned up. I've got some news."

He went to the bunkhouse wondering what the news could be. He felt sweaty and dusty. He grabbed some clean clothes out of his foot locker and took a shower. Ten minutes later, feeling clean and refreshed, he walked across to the house. Mully was sprawled just inside the door when he came in. Irene wasn't in the kitchen. She must have heard him open the door.

"Grab a soda or something," she shouted. "I'll be there in a jiff."

He popped open a Mountain Dew and took it out onto the front porch. There was a slight breeze rustling the trees and it felt comfortable in the shade. He sat in a wooden rocker, put his feet up on the rail and took a sip. He pulled his notebook out of his shirt pocket and laid it on the coffee table. He was ready to report on the fences.

A few minutes later Irene came out carrying a tall glass of lemonade and a bowl of mixed nuts.

"Help yourself," she said. "Have a good day?"

"I made a diagram like you said." Nodding toward the notebook, he said, "It's written down in here. There's a few places need fixing, but the fence is pretty well up all around."

"We'll have to get the repairs made before Friday. Mr. Montoya's in town. Should be a few loads of cattle coming then, or Saturday."

"I was wondering. I didn't see any cattle," he said.

"There'll be plenty next week. See anything interesting?"

"I did see a couple coyotes. And a lot of prairie dogs."

"Bet Mully ignored them, right?"

"Well, she got out of the Jeep after one prairie dog, then pretty much ignored the rest. She watched the coyotes but didn't do anything until they were out of sight."

"I'll tell you about the prairie dogs," Irene said. "When Mully was a pup, I was out in that corner where the prairie dog town is. Mully took off after the first one she saw. When it went down a hole, she chased another one. She kept that up for a couple of hours. She got so tired I had to pick her up and put her back in the truck. She hasn't showed much inclination to chase the little varmints since."

"Well, it didn't seem like she wanted to chase the coyotes either," Lleyellyn said.

Irene smiled at that. Then after a pause, said, "Well she's pretty much had her fill of coyotes, too. But she's still hell on rabbits."

"She's a nice dog," he said, looking at Irene.

Irene nodded.

"Keeps us company. Good dog to have around."

They sat there, sipping their beverages watching the occasional passing vehicle.

"I told you I had some news," Irene said. "I talked to your grandmother today. She called me to see how you're doing. Seems awfully nice."

He looked at Irene who gave him a reassuring smile.

"There's a big manhunt for your stepfather going on, but they haven't found him yet."

He didn't reply at first, but then asked, "How is she doing? My grandmother, I mean."

"She sounded about as good as can be expected. Little worried about you. Wants you to stay away from Minnesota as long as he's on the loose."

Lleyellyn thought about this. He wouldn't know where to look for Mal. He knew Mal grew up on the Mississippi. A regular "river rat." And he had been a Green Beret, seen combat. He could hide out forever.

"If I knew where he was I'd go get him," he said. "But I don't."

oOo

Irene took a casserole dish out of the refrigerator and put it in the oven. Then she sat down across from Shay.

"Your grandmother wanted me to tell you that your mother had some life insurance through her job. You're the sole beneficiary. About ten thousand dollars, she said."

He sat there not saying anything. He had never heard anything about life insurance before, wasn't really sure what life insurance was.

"She'll send the claim forms to you here. Said she'd put

them in the mail today."

Getting no response to this news, Irene changed the subject. "What about the fences?"

"There's only about three places that need fixing. I was able to stand the fence up in one place where two posts were pulled out. Below a little dam by the windmill. Got too wet I think. I've got the places marked in the notebook."

"We'll worry about that later, probably go out and do the fixin' tomorrow. Mr. Montoya is gone. I can help with the repairs, or at least give you some directions if you've never mended fence before."

Lleyellyn grabbed a handful of nuts and washed them down with a sip of his Dew. Irene was getting up to put some dog food in Mully's dish when the phone rang.

"Grab that, will you, hon?" she said.

He picked up the phone. Montoya was on the line.

"Say," he said, "would you go out to my room and get my address book. It is on the shelf under the phone next to the bed. I'll call you back in five minutes or so. I need you to look up a number for me."

"Sure," he started to reply, but Montoya hung up before he had a chance to say anything more.

"That was Mr. Montoya," he told Irene. "He wants me to get his address book. He'll call back in a few minutes"

Irene stopped him before he reached the door.

"You'll need a key. He keeps his room locked." She went into the living room and came back with the key. "Lock it when you're done."

He approached the door to Montoya's room. The key fit smoothly and the door opened quietly.

The curtains were closed and the room was dark. He flipped on the light. He wasn't surprised that the room was neat and clean. The single bed was tightly made. Several books on his desk were stacked squarely. The floor gleamed with fresh polish. A large, framed bullfight poster was on the wall above the bed. He saw the address book under the phone where Montoya said it would be. As he picked it up he glanced at the framed certificates on the wall behind the desk. The biggest one featured a bronze gavel in relief with a certificate to Manuel Patrick Montoya for his services as President of the Granite City Jaycees.

There were many other certificates lined up on the wall in identical black frames. Lleyellyn looked closer. There was a certificate for completing a Refrigeration course. Another for Advanced Keyboarding. Others for Landscaping. Telephone Installation. Conversational Spanish. Television Repair. English Literature II. And several more. Algebra II. Horticulturist I. Introduction to Bovine Disease Prevention. Digital Photography. Every certificate bore fancy script with the words "Granite City" prominently displayed. Shay wasn't sure where Granite City was, but he was impressed with the wide-range of Montoya's interests and education.

He returned from the bunk house and walked into the kitchen as the phone started to ring.

Irene was standing by the sink. She inclined her head toward the phone. He picked it up. It was Montoya.

"I need the number for ... look in the Ds," Montoya said. "D. O. C. See it?"

"Yes, sir," he said, and read off the number.

"Okay. Thanks," Montoya said. "Tell Irene I'll call her soon as I get the first load lined up and ready to roll."

He cut short the call without waiting for Lleyellyn's reply.

Irene looked up as he put the phone down.

"Said he'd call you when the first load is ready to roll," Lleyellyn said, before adding, "Is he okay? Him calling the doc, and all, I mean."

Irene didn't say anything at first. She checked the oven, and set two places at the table.

"That wasn't his doctor," she said. "It was the number for the dee oh cee. Department of Corrections. He needs to get in touch with his parole agent. He has a new one. Must have forgotten the number."

He let this sink in, but didn't say anything. He poured them each a glass of milk and sat down at the table when Irene took the steaming dish out of the stove and placed it between them on a wooden cutting board.

"Mr. Montoya is an interesting man. I'll tell you about him. Fact is, I have all the confidence in the world in him."

During the meal she detailed Montoya's history and her own. Lleyellyn never mentioned that he had already learned some of it from Montoya.

Irene had grown up on a ranch and had gone to high school some thirty miles away in Miles City. Montoya's father was the foreman on a big cattle spread north of town. They had gone to the same high school. Irene was two years ahead of Montoya, and hadn't really known him very well in those days. She told him that she had come to be a sexual assault counselor fair and square because she had been raped in high school. The assailant was the son of a wealthy ranch owner, Montoya's father's boss.

There was a trial. The defendant's friends testified for him and against her and he was acquitted even though everyone knew he was guilty. Irene didn't know it then, but Montoya and the ranch owner's son had never been close.

A lot of people thought the ranch owner's son got away with the rape. There was strong community sentiment in Irene's favor and against her attacker. His father sent him away after the trial. He went off to college in South Dakota. Somehow, Montoya found out and traced him to Grand Forks.

The ranch owner's son, the rapist, was found castrated.

Montoya never denied doing it. He was convicted of first degree assault and sentenced to 30 years in prison. He was sent to the South Dakota State Prison in Sioux Falls. They call it "Granite City." He was a model prisoner. Took a lot of classes. Was president of the Granite City Jaycees and editor of the prison newspaper, *The Insider.*

"I had never talked to Mr. Montoya about my attacker and hadn't seen him since high school. One day when I was in college I wrote him a letter just to see how he was," Irene said. "He wrote back, and we corresponded regularly for over twenty years.

"When it was time for him to be released, I offered him a job here at the ranch. He's been my foreman ever since. Over nine years now."

Lleyellyn had listened in silence, taking occasional bites of the hot dish.

"That explains the certificates on his walls."

CHAPTER TEN

May 23

Lleyellyn sat down at the table and watched as Irene pulled a breakfast casserole from the oven.

"I hope you like eggs," Irene said.

As he was about to reply, they heard a loud diesel-powered truck pull into the drive and stop next to the house.

She went to the door and looked out.

"Dang," she said. "They aren't due until tomorrow."

He got up to see what was going on. A semi loaded with several rows of bright blue portable toilets painted with the *Johnny on the Spot* logo in blaze-pink lettering on the sides sat idling next to the house. A pickup pulling a forklift on a trailer was just turning into the drive behind it.

"Let's see what's going on," Irene said.

They walked down the back steps and approached the semi just as the driver opened the door and climbed down.

"Mornin', Ma'am," he said. "Not too early for you, am I?"

"To tell you the truth, I wasn't expecting you until later in the week," Irene said. "Did you talk to Mr. Montoya?"

"Well, I just got instructions from my boss to bring these beauties out here. I didn't talk to Mr. Montana, or whoever. Just told to load 'em up, and haul 'em out."

"I'll be right back. Lou Ellen, come in with me, will you?"

Back in the kitchen, Irene said, "I'll need you to keep an eye on the unloading of those toilets."

Then she left him standing there as she went into the living room and rummaged around in a cabinet. He was helping himself to a spoonful of Irene's egg casserole when she returned, unfolding a diagram.

"Here's the layout for the port-a-potties. We'll go out and show them this diagram. You keep an eye on them to make sure they follow the plan. Okay?"

"Sure," he said, taking the paper diagram from Irene and laying it out on the kitchen table. He studied it for a moment.

"I just need to know where the starting point is," he said. "Otherwise, looks straight forward to me."

He followed Irene outside. She approached the driver and spread the diagram out on the fender.

"Here's the location plan," she said. "I need these things lined up in two straight lines just like shown here," she said, pointing to the drawing. "We'll show you where the first one goes." Then she looked up at the driver, and flashed a brief smile. "My acting foreman here, Mr. Shay, will be around to make sure that things go smoothly. He's the one to talk to if you have questions."

Then Irene reached over and gently took Lleyellyn by the elbow.

"Come back inside for a minute, will you?" she said. "Wait for Mr. Shay," she said to the driver. "He'll be out in a sec."

In the kitchen Irene insisted that he eat more of his breakfast. As he ate some more, Irene filled him in on the details.

"Mr. Montoya should be here to supervise," she started. "I'm not sure where he is. He's never been gone overnight like last night. You keep an eye on things. I'm going into Miles City to see if I can find him. It isn't like him. He's always kept me informed of his whereabouts."

She watched him eat for a few moments, then explained some more.

The movie production company had arranged to lease the entire ranch for the season. Irene had to keep the grass un-grazed. The movie was about a cattle drive on the Chisholm Trail. The actual cattle drive was going to be filmed on the ranch. Several big stars were involved, but she wasn't sure who.

The producers had arranged for long-horned cattle to be trucked to the ranch next week. Two thousand or more were expected. The wranglers were going to be housed in a tent city and motor homes to the northwest of the house. The portable outhouses were just the prelude. Mobile homes for offices and kitchens were due by the end of the week. Temporary electric fences were going to be installed.

Filming was going to last for several weeks, or as long as it would take. The director planned to wait until there were rain and lightning storms before filming ended.

"Believe me, Lou Ellen," Irene told him, "they are paying me a bundle and they're obligated to put everything back in order when they get done. They've posted a performance bond."

He finished eating and went outside to talk to the driver. Then he got the Jeep. The trucks followed him beyond the barn and the other buildings. He stopped, got out and approached the semi-driver.

"Start the first row here and run the rows north and south. The boss wants you to put two of them off to themselves at the far end. Reserved for the ladies."

"Sure thing. We'll space them about five feet apart. The two rows will be facing each other. Okay?" the driver asked.

Lleyellyn wasn't sure if this is what Irene exactly wanted, but it sounded okay to him.

"That'll work," he said.

The forklift was being unloaded from the trailer behind the pickup when he returned to the house in the Jeep. Irene was just coming out of the back door, Mully following at her heels.

"Hon," she said, "I'm going to run into town. I'll locate Mr. Montoya, and get him back here. Think you can fix those fences by yourself?"

The truth be known, he had never repaired fences. Realizing that Irene had other things on her mind, he said, "Sure. No problem."

"The tools and everything else you'll need are in the shed in the back of the supply building. You better take some Sac-Crete to anchor any loose posts in that draw and near the prairie dogs."

Irene opened the pickup door and told Mully to hop in, then she climbed in, said "See you later," and started her truck.

He could see that three of the portable toilets were already lined up. Looked like they were following the plan.

Before he could turn the Jeep around and head for the supply shed, he saw Irene stop and get out of her truck. She gave him a wave and motioned him over. He drove the Jeep up alongside her and stopped.

"I think you'd better try and get the fence fixed, then get back here as soon as you can. I'm afraid there will be more trucks pulling in at any time. I'd like you here to keep an eye on the place."

Seeing the puzzled look on his face, Irene added, "Just use the diagram in the living room I showed you. Do the best you can to make sure they set up the tents and stuff in the right places. I'll be back as soon as I can."

Irene got back in her pickup and started forward. He watched her go halfway down the driveway, then he drove over to the tool shed. He opened the door and looked around. Mentally making up a supply list, he loaded several sacks of quick concrete mix, a post hole digger, a spool of wire and other tools and supplies into the back of the Jeep. He added two empty five-gallon plastic pails he saw stacked near the door. As an after-thought, he went to the bunk house and after feeling around in the bottom of his duffel bag, retrieved his grandfather's fencing tool he'd been carrying around since he left home, the one he had used to cut down the railroad's copper wire. When the Jeep was loaded, he started retracing the route he had taken the day before when he had checked the fence line.

At his first stop, he took a lopper and trimmed back the brush along the fence where he had noted some fallen limbs the day before. He spent about ten minutes cutting back the limbs and stacking them well away from the fence. He inspected the posts and wire and pounded in two or three loose staples.

He reached the corner where the prairie dogs were and stopped. The fence looked good, but he remembered one of the posts was a bit wobbly in the ground. He took a shovel from the Jeep, and checked the posts near the prairie dog excavations. When he found one that wiggled or seemed loose, he shoveled an eight-to-ten inch hole around the base of the post, then proceeded on. Four of the posts required this treatment.

He continued north along the fence to the stock tank and windmill he had seen the day before. Without wasting time, he filled the two five-gallon pails with water and put them in the back of the Jeep. He drove carefully back toward the fence, trying keep the water from sloshing out.

The forked limb he had used to brace the fence was still in place with the wire intact.

He took out the post hole digger and walked down the wash to the fence line. He dug two holes directly below the fence posts that had been pulled from the ground and were dangling from three strands of barbed wire. He pulled out the forked limb he had used the day before, and put the bottom ends of the old posts in the holes. The tension in the wires kept the posts partially suspended above the holes.

Lleyellyn carefully lifted a sack of concrete and balanced it on the top of one of the posts. It was heavy enough to force the post down into the hole. He did the same with the other dangling post.

Next, he emptied one of the pails and mixed a sack of quick setting pre-mixed concrete. He poured the wet cement into the holes he had dug around the posts, using up the entire sack of mix.

Satisfied that the two posts would stay in place once the concrete set, he went back to the stock tank, filled both buckets, and drove back to the prairie dog town. He mixed another batch of cement and poured it around the base of the posts where he had shoveled out depressions. It took two sacks of mix to finish the job, but it didn't take long.

When he got back to the place below the windmill, he removed the sacks of concrete from the tops of two posts and tried to move the posts. They were solidly imbedded and didn't budge. The fast-setting cement had done its job. He checked the wire, tightened several staples, and was satisfied the fence was strong and tight.

Finally he got back in the Jeep and retraced his way back to the house. The whole job had taken less than three hours.

As he approached the building site he could see that the lines of portable toilets were all in place like two lines of honor guards, standing at attention. There was another semi parked next to the house and a large shirtless man in blue bib overalls was sitting on the kitchen steps smoking a cigarette.

He pulled up in front of the semi and stepped out of the Jeep.

"Hi there," he said. "My name's Shay, can I help you?"

The truck driver looked at him, took an exaggerated puff on his cigarette, and flipped it on the ground.

"I'm looking for the boss," he said. "I've got some tents to unload. The set-up crew will be here soon."

Lleyellyn stuck out his hand and the truck driver shook it.

"I'm the guy in charge. Acting foreman," he said. "I can show you where to put the tents." Then after a pause, "What kind of tents you got?"

"Two twenty-four by forty-eight footers. One's the chow hall. Other one might be an office, I'm not sure."

"Okay," he said, before getting Irene's diagram and spreading it out on the hood of the Jeep. He checked the diagram, then showed it to the driver.

"The mess hall has to be on the far side of the portable johns. At least forty yards to the west. I'll drive over and put a stake in the ground. That'll be for the southwest corner of the tent, okay?"

"You bet. I'll pull over there in a minute," the driver said. "Say, can I use your bathroom?"

He wasn't sure if Irene would appreciate strangers using the bathrooms in the house or in the bunk house.

"No problem," he said, pointing to the twin lines of brightly painted out-houses. "Help yourself. We've got enough to go around."

After putting a stake in the ground to mark the starting point for the mess tent, Shay went to the bunkhouse, showered and changed into clean clothes. As an afterthought, he put on the belt with the silver buckle Buck had given him and the wide-brimmed hat he had bought for the rodeo.

The entire time he was getting cleaned up he thought about his mother and about her killer. He wondered if Mal was still on the loose.

Lleyellyn found the folded up paper he had placed in his wallet with the investigator's name and number. He wanted to find out if they were closing in on Mal. He called the Winona County Sheriff's office.

"Law Enforcement Center," a female voice answered.

"How can I direct your call?"

"Investigator Wilson, please."

There was a short pause before a crisp, no-nonsense voice said, "Wilson. Can I help you?"

He cleared his throat. He wasn't sure how to begin. The murder never left his mind, even when he kept busy with the jobs around the ranch.

"This is Lleyellyn Shay. I'm wondering if you've learned any more about my mother's death. Have you caught Mal?"

While he waited for an answer, it sounded like the investigator had put his hand over the mouthpiece and was talking to someone else. He heard indistinguishable mumbled voices.

"Sorry, Mr. Shay, I was talking to a deputy. We've got some leads. Haven't made an arrest yet. Someone reported seeing him near Latch Island yesterday."

Lleyellyn considered this information.

"He used to talk about growing up on the river. Used to camp out. Fish. Trap, and stuff." he said. "Told my mom he knew the river better than anyone."

"There's a lot of manpower out looking for him. It's only a matter of time and we'll find him," the investigator said.

Then, after what Shay thought was the sound of swallowing, coffee, perhaps or a soft drink, the deputy asked, "How you doing?"

"Well, I've been busy. Irene, my boss, she's got me keeping an eye on things and repairing fences." He shifted his position, then less convincingly, added, "I'm doing okay."

"Listen, kid. Lleyellyn. We're putting a lot of effort into finding your mother's killer. I'll call you at the ranch there in Montana when we get him," the investigator said. "And you call me anytime if you need to talk to someone ... or need an update."

"Thanks," he said softly, then, managed to speak up and

add, "Good luck. Hope you catch the bastard soon."

He walked out the back door and watched the kitchen tent going up. He could see the center poles were in place, the white vinyl-coated canvas was draped loosely around the perimeter. Several young men about his age were putting up side supports and pounding in stakes. He thought everything was going according to plan. They seemed to be working fast and efficiently.

He entered the kitchen with the idea of getting a Mountain Dew out of the refrigerator and making a sandwich. The telephone startled him from his thoughts about Mal being on the loose when it rang just as he was about to take the first sip of the cold soda.

"Hello."

"Who is this?" a male voice said.

"Lleyellyn. Lleyellyn Shay," he said as he suddenly recognized the caller's voice. "Is that you, Mr. Montoya?"

"Yes. Say, is Irene there?"

"No. She left about an hour ago. Went into Miles City looking for you."

There was no immediate reply from Montoya. He took another sip and holding the receiver to his ear with a cocked shoulder, opened the refrigerator and took out some luncheon meat and a package of sliced cheddar.

Finally Montoya spoke. "Irene won't be able to find me. Try and get her on her cell phone. Tell her I'll be back there in a few days."

"I could look up her cell number for you," he said.

"No, you call her. I don't want to talk to her right now. There's something I've got to do. Pass on the message," Montoya said.

He thought Montoya seemed to be in a hurry. He hung up before Lleyellyn could reply and before saying good-bye.

Irene had phone numbers listed on a card tacked up next to the phone. He found a number next to the words *"my cell number"* and dialed it.

"Irene," she said after the second ring. "How're you doing as my acting foreman?" *She has caller ID*, he thought. He could hear a smile in her voice.

"Okay, I think. Fence is fixed pretty good. Biffies are all set up. They're almost done putting up a big mess tent and there's another one, too. I think it'll go up next."

"Great," Irene said.

"Reason I'm calling, Mr. Montoya just called. Asked me to call you. Said he'll be home in a few days. Something he has to do."

"Did he say where he was?"

"No."

There was silence on the line as Irene seemed to be considering this information.

"Well, I called a few people around town," she said. "He was here in Miles City. Spent a couple of hours at the Public Library on the internet. The librarian knows me. Knows about Mr. Montoya – his story. She said he was downloading news articles about a murder. When he asked her to print out some copies she saw they were articles about a recent murder in Winona, Minnesota. Your mother's murder, it seems."

"Why?" he said. "I don't understand."

"Lleyellyn, I'm not real sure I do either. What I think is, he's finding out about the murder. Wants to make sure your stepfather Mal gets the justice he has coming. Just like he saw to it that the guy that assaulted me got what Montoya thought was justice."

Lleyellyn didn't say anything. *Montoya hardly knows me*, he thought. *He didn't know my mother at all.*

Irene interrupted his thoughts.

"Don't do anything. I'll be back this afternoon. We'll talk about it then."

He didn't think Montoya would be able to find Mal. As far as he knew, Montoya had never been to Minnesota or on the Mississippi River. He had spent all of his adult life in prison or at Irene's ranch.

He would look like an outsider in Winona if he showed up there.

He wondered if the investigator was telling him everything. He needed to talk to someone. He called his grandmother. She was glad to hear from him. He realized that she must have talked to Irene again, when she asked him about being the interim ranch foreman.

"Who told you that?" he asked.

"Why, son, didn't Mr. Montoya tell you? He's called me two or three times to see how the manhunt's going. He called this morning, in fact."

"He didn't say anything to me," he said. "What did he tell you?"

"Well, he said you were doing good working at the ranch and filling in when he was at some convention or workshop, or something. Mostly, he seemed concerned about Mal being still on the run. Wanted to know what I'd heard."

"What'd you tell him?"

"Well, let me think. A deputy stopped by. Said Mal had been seen at Latch Island. Probably stole a boat, he said. Flat bottomed aluminum one. With an outboard motor. You know, sorta like the one he kept in the yard."

"Anything else?"

"Hon, you sound like one of the sheriff's investigators. Don't know what else I said. Let me think. I did say he was probably holed up on one of the islands between Winona and the Trempealeau Refuge, I think."

"You told Montoya that?"

"Yes. Yes, I think I did. Told him that Mal was raised a river rat and knows the back channels of the river backwards and forwards."

"What did Montoya say?"

"Not much, really. Hoped they'd catch him. Soon. Said attacking and killing a woman was a terrible crime and he shouldn't be able to get away from justice. He seemed nice. Just concerned. He must really like you."

He didn't respond at first, until his grandmother asked if he was still on the line.

"Yeah, Grandma. I was just thinking. Call me if you hear anything. I've gotta get back to work."

As he hung up, he realized Irene was right. Montoya could be, in fact probably was, looking for Mal.

oOo

Lleyellyn went outside. He saw the mess tent was now completely up. Final adjustments were being made on the tie-downs. He got in the Jeep and drove over to talk to the crew chief.

"Tent's bigger than I thought," Shay said. "You sure got it up fast."

"We've had a lot of practice. Where's the other one go?"

"What's it going to be used for?" Lleyellyn asked.

"Day room. Personnel office. That kind of thing. Where the cast and crew meet to get their assignments, rehearse, shoot the shit and relax, you know."

Lleyellyn picked up the plot drawing and studied it for a moment. None of the squares were marked "day room" or "personnel office" or anything similar.

"Well, put it directly west of this chow hall tent. Easy for people to eat and go next door to the day room. Could you line it up square with this one, maybe forty to fifty feet space between the two?"

"You're the boss," the crew chief said with a grin. "We'll have it up in no time. An hour, hour and a half. Tops."

Shay turned to get back in the Jeep when the guy said, "We'll be back tomorrow with a few smaller tents and a crew to install some electric fence for the horses. You gonna be here to show us the layout?"

He looked back over his shoulder and said, "Should be. If not, the boss lady herself will be here. Or maybe Mr. Montoya, the foreman. See you tomorrow."

oOo

He got restless waiting for Irene to return.

He went to the storage shed and carefully cut the flaps off several white-colored cardboard boxes and took them to the house. Using a felt marker he found in the drawer next to the cutlery, he neatly printed out several signs on the cardboard.

OFF LIMITS

He was going to write "Except to full time ranch personnel" but he wasn't sure how to spell personnel, so he wrote:

FULL TIME RANCH RESIDENTS ONLY!!

Then he took a few thumb tacks and a roll of scotch tape he had spotted in a kitchen drawer and put up a sign on both the front and back doors of the house and another on the bunk house door. He added one to the supply shed door and the final one on the barn door.

While he was in a sign-making mood, he made up several small placards offering Tole's "association" saddle for sale. *$950. Like New!* He tacked one near the entry to the mess tent under one of the black and white photographs of Tole on the horse at the rodeo. He drew an arrow pointing to the saddle and wrote: *THIS IS THE SADDLE! $950!* He also taped two signs about the saddle at the head of each line of portable latrines.

He was sitting on the front porch nursing a Mountain Dew and another bologna and cheese sandwich when Irene pulled in. She let Mully out and the dog ran over to Lleyellyn wagging her tail. He rubbed her ears and patted her back, said "Nice girl!" a couple of times and then walked over to greet Irene who was just getting out of the big Dodge.

"Hon, would you get the box of groceries on the front seat? I've got to talk to you."

The dog stayed outside eating a piece of the sandwich he had tossed her. Irene and he went in the house.

"Sit down, will you? I'll put these things away. Pizza okay for tonight?" Irene said.

"Sure. Love pizza," he said. "Need any help?"

"No. I can do it. By the way, like the sign. Any special reason for it?" she asked.

"Well, a truck driver wanted to use your bathroom. I just figured with nobody around, it was a good idea to put signs up. I put another one on the front door and some on the bunk house and several other places, too."

"Good thinking," Irene said. "Let's go in. Heat up the pizza. I want to talk to you."

When the pizza was ready, they sat down in the kitchen.

"What I want to talk to you about is this. Mr. Montoya is probably on his way to Minnesota to try and track down the guy killed your mother. It's like what he did after I was assaulted back in high school. He has this, I don't know what – sense of justice or vengeance or something."

"How'll he ever find Mal? He's never even been to Minnesota or in the Mississippi back waters. That's where Mal will be."

"No, he hasn't been back there. And I don't know if he can find him. If he does, I don't know what he'll do."

"Kill him, you think?"

Irene paused. "I don't know. He could. He has an ingrained sense of right and wrong. He did it before, sort of. But what I'm worried about is his parole violation. He can't leave Montana while on parole. If he gets found anywhere outside Montana he'll probably be sent back to prison, maybe for the rest of his life."

"Why would he risk it?"

"I'm not sure. He's been a model parolee. His agent doesn't check up on him very often and she just saw him two days ago. But if he gets violated, then he'll be in deep trouble, I'm sure of it," Irene said. "I suppose he doesn't expect to get caught."

"I made two calls. I talked to the investigator and my grandmother. I'll pay you back for the calls...."

Irene held up a hand, interrupting. "Now, hon. Don't worry about the calls. One of the perks of being acting foreman."

"They both said that Mal's probably hiding out on an island in the Mississippi. He stole a boat and motor. He knows that area better than anyone. Grew up there. And he learned survival skills as a Green Beret or Ranger, or something. Mr. Montoya will never find him. Maybe nobody will."

"You might be right. But he'll try. If he gets ID'd back in Minnesota he'll really be up a creek."

They ate the rest of the pizza in silence.

He ran through what they had been talking about in his mind. *Montoya's a strange guy to figure out.*

"Say, hon, almost forgot to tell you. One of the movie stuntmen bought your friend's saddle while you were getting cleaned up this morning. Paid your asking price."

She handed him an envelope.

"There's nine hundred and fifty dollars in here. He's got the saddle. I found it in the storage room."

"That's great," Lleyellyn said. "Tole'll be happy with that."

When he took his dish to the sink, Irene looked at him, a serious expression of concern on her face.

"I think you'll have to go to Minnesota and try and locate Mr. Montoya before he gets himself in trouble."

CHAPTER ELEVEN

May 24

Lleyellyn packed his clothes. Before going to bed he wrote out a check for $950 and put it an envelope he stamped and addressed to Tole Winters in Wisconsin. He considered subtracting the money he had loaned Tole at the hospital, but thought they were close to even since Tole had paid for the motel. He added a note about a stuntman buying the saddle and inquired about his friend's injured shoulder.

He planned to mail it the first chance he got.

Shay woke up early, looked out the window and saw Irene leave the house and start her pickup. He got dressed quickly. When he came out of the bunkhouse, Mully ran toward him. She was eager to go for a ride, as usual.

"Morning, Mully," he said, carrying his duffle bag to the Dodge and putting it in the back end.

The dog squeezed in ahead of him as he opened the passenger door.

"Ready to go?" Irene said. "Mully sure is."

"Guess so," he said uncertainly. "Musta overslept."

He stifled a yawn, and added, "Just how am I going to get to Winona?"

As they turned on the road heading for Miles City, Irene said, "I got up earlier than usual. Called around. Trucker's going to meet us in town. Mail hauler. Contract guy. Seattle to Detroit.

Arrow Drayage, I think. Used to haul cattle around here. Said he'd take you east along I-94. Passing through St. Paul. That's pretty close to home, isn't it?"

"Winona's south. Two, maybe two and a half hours from St. Paul," he said.

He wondered how long it would take to get to the Twin Cities and how he'd get from there to Winona. Irene seemed to read his thoughts.

"There's a relief driver. They'll drive straight on through. Expect to be in the St. Paul area about eight or nine tomorrow morning."

She looked over at him and gave him a reassuring smile which he could barely make out in the glow from the dashboard lights.

"They'll get on the horn when they get to Minnesota. Find you another truck driver, or somebody, heading towards Winona. Told me it's no big deal."

Lleyellyn didn't think it could be that easy. He didn't say anything as he stared ahead down the deserted road. Irene interrupted his reverie.

"I've got your pay here in cash and some extra so you can get a motel, eat, buy what you need."

When he didn't reply, Irene continued, "When you get to Winona, make some inquiries. Look around. Mr. Montoya kind of stands out. I've never seen him wear anything but his khaki clothes and matching hat. If he's around people should remember."

"I'll check around town," he said. "But what do I do if I find him? How can I get him to come back to the ranch?"

Irene didn't reply at first, just stared ahead down the road. Finally she said, "Just try and get him to call me before he does something he'll regret."

oOo

The eastern sky had a faint early morning glow as they reached Miles City. Irene looked over at him. He had been half asleep for about an hour.

"We've got time for breakfast," she said as she pulled into the lot next to a café. It wasn't until they stepped down from the pickup and let the dog sniff around and relieve itself that Lleyellyn recognized the place. They were right across from the motel where he and Tole had stayed during the rodeo.

He followed Irene through the door. The place was full of men. Workmen. Fishermen. Hunters. He looked up as LaDonna Mae came through the swinging kitchen doors carrying a tray stacked with breakfast orders. She didn't see him at first. When she did, she smiled, put the tray down on the counter, and came up to him.

"Lou Ellen!" she said, giving him a kiss full on the lips. Someone hooted. Everyone was watching them.

Irene cleared her throat.

"I see you two have met," she deadpanned.

He blushed.

LaDonna Mae spoke up. "This is the guy I was telling you about, Irene. We met last week. I didn't know you knew him."

"Well, it's a small world," Irene said. "You better serve these other bozos or there'll be a riot,'" she said, gesturing to the seated breakfast crowd, and smiling. "We'll take that booth over there. We can fill you in later."

When they sat down, Shay said, "You must know LaDonna Mae, huh?"

Irene looked at him, then glanced at the menu.

"Well, it appears obvious that you do," she said.

He wondered if he should explain how he met LaDonna Mae.

"Let's order," Irene said. "You have a long trip ahead of you."

He was staring at the menu, not really seeing anything, when LaDonna Mae came back to their table. She smiled at them and took their orders. He ordered the sausage and eggs special.

Irene just said, "The usual," and winked at the waitress.

"I'll get this order in and stop back and talk when I bring your coffee. And a Mountain Dew."

Lleyellyn watched her walk toward the kitchen. She turned and flashed him a smile. He looked up to see Irene grinning back at him.

"She's a nice gal, hon. I think she's got a thing for you."

He looked down at the table, slightly embarrassed. Then he looked Irene squarely in the eye and said, "Yes. She's very nice. I do really like her. A lot."

It didn't take long before LaDonna Mae was bringing their breakfasts and beverages on a tray.

The crowd was busy eating. Another waitress was walking around filling coffee cups.

"Scoot over, Lou Ellen," she said. "What're you doing back in town so soon?"

Irene ate and watched him and LaDonna Mae as he brought her up to date. He told her about hitching a ride with Irene. Getting hired to work on her ranch. Finding out about his mother's murder. He didn't mention anything about Montoya. Finally, he said, "I'm going to Minnesota to tie up a few loose ends."

LaDonna Mae looked at him intently through the whole narration. She put her hands around his arm.

"Lou Ellen," she started. "Your mother. That's horrible."

He patted her hand.

"Yes," he said. "I know."

The cook shouted, "Order up!" and LaDonna Mae slid out of the booth, picked up her tray and hurried to the kitchen. He and Irene finished their meals in silence.

"It's about time to go," Irene said. "I've got to powder my nose. Be back in a sec."

He caught LaDonna Mae's eye and signaled for the check. She brought it over and handed it to him.

"I'll be back," he said. "I think I have a real job at Irene's ranch. I'll let you know when I get back."

He gave her a hug. The restaurant crowd watched. Silent this time.

"If anyone asks, don't tell them I'm going back to Minnesota. I want to keep that quiet. Okay?"

"No problem. Your secret's safe with me. Now, be careful," LaDonna Mae said. "I'll miss you."

He left the money on the table and left. He was waiting for Irene in the pickup when she came out.

"Now, Lleyellyn. You didn't have to pick up the tab," she said.

"I wanted to."

oOo

It was a little after six when Irene pulled up next to the truck pumps at the Petro Truck Plaza on the edge of town just off the interstate. They no more than got out of the pickup when a semi pulled up next to the canopy and the driver got out.

"Irene!" the driver said. "You get better lookin' every day."

Irene and the driver shook hands.

"This piece of work is your chauffeur. Dave Bramer. Lleyellyn Shay," she said by way of introduction.

They shook hands and exchanged small talk for a minute or two, then Bremer said, "We'd best be on our way."

Shay climbed into the passenger side of the cab. He looked back and saw Irene hand the driver an envelope which he stuffed in his shirt pocket.

They pulled out of the truck stop, crossed the overpass, and turned right onto the east-bound lanes of the I-94.

Finally, Bremer spoke up. "I'm hauling packaged mail. This is the daily Seattle to Milwaukee run. Two drivers relay eight hours each from Seattle; then I take over. I drive eight hours and then I am relieved. Truck gets into the Twin Cities in about fifteen hours, give or take. Depending on the weather. Traffic. I'll hand the rig over to the next driver. Max'll take you the rest of the way."

"Well, I sure appreciate you having me along," Shay said.

"Irene's quite the gal. She asked me to take you. I never say no to that gal. She's done a lot for me and my family over the years," Bremer said.

He thought this over.

"I haven't known her very long. She's already helped me out a lot."

As they settled into the steady seventy-five mile an hour flow of traffic, Lleyellyn had a chance to look around. From the cab they seemed to have a bird's eye view of the traffic and the scenery. Off to the side of the road Lleyellyn saw several herds of grazing antelope.

"This is pronghorn county," Bremer said. "In all the time I've been driving this route I've never seen a dead one along the road. See them all the time but they stay away from traffic."

The driver reached over and adjusted several knobs. The CB radio crackled into clarity. Shay listened to the chatter.

Bremer picked up the mike and spoke: "Breaker, breaker. Postman here. What you got east of Ranch Forty Road? Over."

Almost immediately there was a reply. "Postman. Clear the past twenty miles. Scales closed. Buffalo Shorty, out."

oOo

The driver kept up a steady stream of banter. Shay listened, making brief replies and nodding as the driver talked about his elk hunting trips, his favorite baseball team and his family. Finally Lleyellyn nodded off, put to sleep by the steady chatter of the driver and the drone of the diesel engine.

"Hey there partner," Bremer said when he started to wake up as Bremer down-shifted and slowed down for a rest area. "Here's where Max takes over," Bremer said as he guided the rig to the truck parking area and slowly pulled in between an orange Schneider National tractor trailer and a J.B. Hunt semi, diagonally parked in a line of twenty or more eighteen-wheelers.

"Rule number one," he said, raising a finger. "Never park next to a livestock hauler." Then still smiling at his joke, added, "You might want to use the facilities. Max isn't one to make unnecessary stops."

When he returned to the truck, Bremer was animatedly talking to a dark-haired diminutive woman wearing a turquoise pantsuit. He guessed she was in her forties.

"Lleyellyn. Meet Maxine. She's taking over from here."

"Call me Max," the woman said smiling at him. "Everyone does." They shook hands, then Max turned to Bremer. "See you on the return trip. Say hello to the missus for me."

"Enjoy the trip," Bremer said to both of them before he walked towards his car parked along the fence behind the row of idling semis. Then he stopped, turned around, and came back.

"I almost forgot."

He pulled out the envelope Irene had given him, took something out, and handed the envelope to Max.

"Irene asked me to give this to you," he said.

Then he looked at Lleyellyn and shook hands with him, palming a folded piece of paper to Lleyellen as he did so.

He opened his hand and saw the folded up bill, the printed "$100" in a corner clearly visible.

"Irene gave me this for the trouble. I enjoyed your company. You'll need it more than I do."

Then he turned and walked to his car.

He wasn't sure what to do, or say. He started to follow Bremer, then stopped and shouted,

"Thanks. Thanks for everything."

Bremer didn't look back, but he gave a little wave with his left hand, then unlocked his car, opened the door and got in. He drove off without a glance in their direction.

He and Max watched Bremer drive off, before Max spoke.

"Need to go to the john? I need a few minutes to adjust the seat and get my stuff stowed."

He told her he had just been to the men's room and asked if he could help any.

She told him, "No." She indicated it would only take a few minutes. "Climb in, then. Get comfortable."

Max adjusted the driver's seat and fastened padded cushions to the seat and back. Then she placed a cooler between the seats and plugged it into the lighter. Finally she arranged a padded box of CDs on top of the cooler and inserted several disks in the stereo.

Before putting the truck in gear she looked at him. She seemed awfully small to be driving such a big truck especially in comparison to Bremer.

"I've been trying to learn Italian. Hope my CDs don't bother you too much. I almost always start out with my Italian language lesson."

"No, Ma'am. Of course not. Won't bother me."

"I hate to waste time when I'm driving. I'm going to Italy later in the year. This might help."

She handed the CD box to him. *Berlitz Conversational*

Italian was printed on the box with a picture of a gondolier.

"I'm replaying the first hour as a refresher. When I get tired of that I usually put on some music. You like opera?" she asked.

He looked at her. "Gee," he said. "I'm not sure I even know what opera is."

"Well, I'll fix that before we reach the Twin Cities."

She put the truck in gear, eased smoothly forward, and flipped on the stereo.

As they left the rest area and pulled onto the interstate, a well-modulated voice recited Italian phrases followed by the English translation.

Maxine listened, then repeated each phrase several times. It was obvious that she had been practicing. Her pronunciation seemed to him to perfectly replicate the announcer's voice.

"You can try it, too," Max invited. "If you want."

He listened and repeated several phrases.

"Hey. Pretty good. *Bene,*" Max said.

They spent the better part of an hour repeating the announcer's careful diction, sometimes individually, sometimes in unison.

"You sound like a pro," Max said. "But that's enough homework for now." She reached over and turned off the stereo. "Recess time. Look in the cooler, will you? Get me a Diet Pepsi, *per favore.*"

He opened the cooler and removed a Diet Pepsi, popped the tab, and handed it to Max.

"Thanks," she said. "Help yourself to whatever you want." He opened the cooler. There was nothing but Diet Pepsi. He took one. He couldn't remember the last time he drank anything other than Mountain Dew.

"'Fraid there isn't too much to choose from," Max said.

"No problem," he said. "Tastes good. *Grazie.*"

As they continued eastbound, Max asked him where he was

going. She said Bremer had told her a few things, but not much.

"I'm heading to Winona. Minnesota," he said. "My Mom died there last week. Murdered, really. By my stepfather. My trip's kind of a secret."

Maxine didn't reply at first. She took a sip of her soft drink, then glanced over at him.

"Well your secret's safe with me," she said, then added, "He in jail?"

"No," he said. "Supposed to be a manhunt going on. No luck yet."

"I don't know Irene," Max said. "From what Bremer told me, she sounds like a nice person."

They drove in silence for a while before Max picked up the CB. Before turning the volume up, she said, "There's a retired driver just up a ways. Pretty much confined to a wheelchair. Keeps up on trucker news by talking on the radio. I always give him a shout when I'm in range."

Maxine adjusted the volume and the squealch, then spoke into the transceiver.

"Hey Doggie, you copy?"

Almost immediately there was a reply.

"Max. Goldarned. Thought I must have missed you today. Still practicing your eye-talian?"

"You betcha," Max said. "What's new today?"

"Steady traffic all day. Nothing too heavy. Reefer flipped onto its side this morning. Forty mile west. Real heavy wind. No injuries, but there was a half-mile of frozen pizzas on the interstate for a while."

"Any of the old timers pass through today?" Max asked.

"Well that husband-wife team from Bismarck came through. They were arguing like they always do, even when talking to me. This is supposed to be their fortieth year on the road together and they're still going strong."

"Haven't killed each other yet, anyway," Max said.

They would have talked longer, but Doggie's voiced started to fade out as the static increased.

"I'll catch you on the flip side," Maxine said and simultaneously turned down the volume and advanced to another CD in the stereo.

"Okay, Lleyellyn, back to school. Music appreciation. Here's an opera for you."

Maxine adjusted the volume and the tone and loud classical music filled the cab.

He listened intently. It didn't sound half bad. The deep bass of the male voice and the high-pitched female soloist were alternating in some foreign language which he assumed was Italian.

The piece lasted a good twenty minutes. Maxine kept her eyes on the road, but he could see her keeping the rhythm by tapping her fingers on the steering wheel.

When the music stopped, Maxine turned the stereo off and said, "What do you think? Be honest now."

"Well," he began, glancing her way. "I thought it was stirring, emotional, but I couldn't understand the words. Were they singing in Italian?"

"Yes. What I played was a scene from the Barber of Seville, one of the classics. It's one of the operas I plan to see when I get to La Scala in Italy. Always one of my favorites."

Seeing that he wasn't too sure what she was talking about, she added, "The La Scala opera house is in Milano. Milan, Italy. It's like the Yankee Stadium of the opera world. Or Wrigley Field. Maybe Carnegie Hall. I bought my tickets about six months ago."

Max talked on about opera. He found himself interested in spite of himself.

"You seem to know a lot about opera," he said when there

was a pause in the discussion.

"Driving truck can get pretty lonely. I try and learn something with these recordings. It sure beats the heck out of back and forth chit-chat on the CB and the usual, if you'll excuse my French, the usual B.S. that many of the guys like to spout."

Up ahead Lleyellyn noticed a camper parked on the shoulder. He saw its brake lights flick on and off. When they got close, the camper suddenly pulled forward and turned across the two east bound lanes right in front of them. Maxine hit the brakes, veered to the right and squeezed by the camper on the shoulder.

"Bruto bastardo!" she shouted, before settling into the right lane and resuming highway speed.

"I don't like to swear. But I'm so surprised at myself. I must be thinking in Italian. I swore in Italian, something I almost never do in English."

"Maybe your lessons are paying off," he said. "And your driving wasn't too shabby either. Damn. I didn't think you'd be able to avoid hitting that idiot."

"I don't think he even saw us," Maxine said. "If he had, he might have hit the brakes hard and then he'd be splattered all over the road."

oOo

As they approached St. Cloud, Minnesota, Maxine picked up her cell phone, scrolled through her index and placed a call.

"I'll find you a ride from the Twin Cities," she said. "I'm going to put this on speaker so you can hear, too."

He heard the sound of a phone ringing coming through the stereo speakers. After two rings a female voice said, "Midwestern Truck Expediters, Darla speaking."

"Darla, this is Max. How're you doing?"

"Great, Max. Good to hear from you. Looking to come back to work for us or you still hauling that junk mail?"

"Same old, same old," Maxine said. "I called you for a favor. I need to find a ride for a friend of mine from the Twin Cities to Winona in about two hours. Got any of your drivers heading that way?"

"I might. I'll check my screen, make a couple of calls. I'll get back to you in a bit. You at your cell?"

"Yes," Max said. "Appreciate it."

At the end of the call, Max told him how Darla had been the dispatcher she used when she was an independent owner-operator.

"I've never met Darla in person, but we've known each other on the phone for fifteen years, at least."

He was going to ask some questions, but the phone rang before he could gather his thoughts.

"Max."

"It's me, Darla. Found a ride. Auto transporter. We call him Gabby. For obvious reasons. Talks your ears off. He'll be at the St. Croix Shell Truck Plaza in Hudson, Wisconsin. Plans to stop there for lunch and depart at one fifteen. That work for you?"

"Sure does. We should get there at about twelve thirty or so, depending on traffic."

"Gabby wants fifty bucks for the trouble. Is that okay?" Darla asked.

"Sure," Maxine said. "And thanks."

"No problem. You'll be able to spot Gabby in the coffee shop. Big guy. Wears a yellow Packer's hat that says *'I'm not Brett'* on the front."

"We'll find him."

"Oh, and another thing, I meant what I said when I said Gabby does like to talk. Ear-plugs might help," the dispatcher said, stifling laughter. "Have a nice trip."

Max looked at him. He shrugged.

"Hey, how bad can it be? I'm impressed how fast you found a ride."

Maxine smiled.

"You'll be in Winona by early this evening."

oOo

Spotting Gabby was easy. He was the only person seated in the professional driver's section of the coffee shop. His yellow *I'm not Brett* cap was on the table in front of him, next to a hot beef sandwich with three scoops of mashed potatoes, all of it covered with thick brown gravy.

"Gabby?" Maxine said.

"Yes, ma'am," he replied. "You my paying passenger for Winona?"

"No. Not me," she replied. "Lleyellyn here is your rider."

"Lleyellyn. Well there's a moniker for you. Okay then. I'll be ready to roll when I finish lunch and visit the little boy's room." He paused, then added, "I'm Gabby."

They exchanged quick handshakes. Lleyellyn's hand was engulfed in Gabby's giant right paw.

"One more thing. Fifty bucks. Who's paying?"

Max pulled a bent envelope from her pants pocket. Lleyellyn recognized it as the one Irene handed to Bremer at the start of the trip. She removed a fifty dollar bill and handed it to Lleyellyn.

"Here's the fare. Give it to Gabby when you get to Winona."

Gabby watched him put the money in his pocket but didn't say anything before turning and taking a dripping fork full of gravy soaked sandwich.

"We'll meet you outside. That your rig with new Buicks on it?" Maxine asked.

Gabby simply nodded and continued eating.

Maxine and Lleyellyn left the restaurant and went into the convenience store section.

"You want anything? Drink? Food?"

"No. I'm good," he said. "Can I get you a Diet Pepsi?"

"Thanks, but no thanks. I've got plenty in the cooler."

Then Max looked at Lleyellyn earnestly and took his hand.

"I enjoyed your company. Here's the rest of the money Bremer gave me. Said it was from Irene."

"No, you keep it. Buy some more opera recordings."

"You'll need it. It was no trouble having you along." Then, as she turned to leave, she added, "That Irene must be some woman. I'd like to meet her someday. Have a good trip."

She walked a few steps, and turned around, a big smile on her face.

"Arrivederci, Lleyellynardo."

He didn't hesitate. Returning the smile, he answered, *"Ciao, Bella. Grazie mille."*

He watched her walk towards the truck parking lot and disappear behind a long line of idling semis. He opened the envelope. There were two fifty dollar bills inside. And a business card.

He took out the card and read it. Maxine "Max" Robbins, Vice President, North American Opera Lovers Club, it read. It also listed her street, telephone and email addresses.

As he walked past a mailbox next to several newspaper racks by the entrance to the truck stop, he remembered his letter to Tole. He dropped the envelope in the box and went looking for Gabby.

"Hop in, son," *I'm not Brett* said, as he walked around the front end of a green Peterbuilt attached to an open trailer of new Buicks.

Shay placed his pack behind the passenger seat, and

climbed aboard. The driver got in and settled behind the wheel.

"Okay son, here's the plan. We're heading west a few miles to I-494, head south a bit, then take US sixty-one all the way down to Winona. Not a freeway, but real scenic."

Lleyellyn was about to say that he had driven the route before, but the driver continued talking before he had the opportunity.

"Usually see eagles along Lake Pepin. Prettiest stretch of the Great River Road. U.S. sixty-one goes from the Canadian border, Thunder Bay, along the north shore of Lake Superior, then follows the Mississippi to the Gulf of Mexico."

He looked over at the driver to see if a response was expected.

Gabby was staring at the road ahead. He didn't glance at Shay, but he did continue talking.

"They say the blues started along route sixty-one in Mississippi. And another thing, they have what some call the longest garage sale in the world along sixty-one, too. From Hastings to Wabasha. Pretty big deal."

He didn't think a reply was expected. The driver picked up the CB and asked about conditions along I-94 to 494 and then down to sixty-one. Someone replied that traffic was down to one lane each way near the 494/61 interchange, but that it was moderate.

"That stretch has been under construction for well over a year," the driver told him. "They're adding a third lane in each direction. The interchange at sixty-one, where 494 crosses the river, is really screwed up. Some law suit or something. Cost over-runs. Delays. Supposed to be done last year. Now, nobody knows."

"Drive this way often?" he tried to interject.

"Different route every day. Haul new vehicles to dealers all over the upper mid-west. New autos. Collector cars. Pickups.

High-end stuff exclusively."

He shot another look at the driver, who kept talking as they took the off-ramp onto south-bound sixty-one.

"Collector cars get special treatment. Enclosed trailers. Protection from the elements. And vandals. Usually one or two cars per load. A lot of collector vehicles are worth big bucks. Million dollars. Maybe more. Had a sixty-two Ferrari last month. Concourse condition. Two point three million."

"Wow," he managed to say, before the driver continued, virtually uninterrupted.

"Last year I hauled a Bugatti Royale to a big-time collector in Nevada. Casino owner. One of two or three in existence. Four million. I kid you not."

As they crossed the Mississippi bridge and slowed down entering Hastings, the driver was going strong.

"Hastings is supposed to be the birthplace of several governors, I've heard. Not sure it's true. St. Peter makes the same claim. I do know it's the county seat of Dakota County. Minnesota's fastest growing. Lot of serious crimes here the past few years. To me, it's a bottleneck. All these damned stoplights. Not truck friendly," he said as he slowed for a red light, and brought the rig to a stop behind a line of cars.

"Toughest place to haul new cars in an open trailer is Chicago. Get off on the wrong exit and most of the windows will be busted out in a few blocks. Bullets. Rocks. Whatever. I try to avoid Chi-town."

"Sounds dangerous," Lleyellyn squeezed in as they continued slowly through town, then turned left where US Sixty 61 veered to the right.

"Short-cut," the driver said. "Up ahead a ways is the Treasure Island Casino. Indian owned. Lots of Twin City folks. Retirees. Big money-maker for the tribe. I've heard it said each registered tribal member gets eleven, twelve thousand dollars a month from the profits. Indians don't work there. Use their money for fooling around. Spend their time spearing wall-eyes. Shooting deer. Dancing at pow-wows. Got it made. Made in the shade."

Lleyellyn wasn't sure how to reply. He realized that what Gabby was saying was bullshit. Finally, to avoid controversy, he said, "Is that a fact. Wow."

As the short-cut joined up with highway sixty-one again and they turned left, Gabby resumed talking.

"Red Wing is next. Real old river town. One of the best-looking river towns in Minnesota. It's another son-of-a-bitch to drive through. We'll pass the correctional facility. Juvenile delinquents. Reform school type of place. Been here since the eighteen hundreds."

He saw the high in-curving chain link fence and the impressive clock tower of the prison. He knew two guys from Winona who had spent some time there. It looked oppressive. There were basketball courts behind the fenced-in yard. They were vacant.

"Say. You must have seen that big bluff back there by the overpass. Called The Barn. Indian myth is that the other half of The Barn is in Winona. Sugar Loaf."

"Oh, yeah. I know it," Lleyellyn said. He had climbed Sugar Loaf, but he didn't get a chance to tell the driver.

"Sugar Loaf has been quarried down to about nothing. Used it to build the courthouse and some banks and stuff. Supposed to have looked like The Barn before they started cutting it up."

Shay didn't respond, but looked over at the driver. *Doesn't he ever shut up?* The driver glanced briefly at Lleyellyn, then continued his spiel.

"We're going to be coming up to Lake Pepin. A wide spot in the Mississippi. Natural lake. Formed by the Chippewa River's sediment. Lotta sail boats. Lots of recreational activity.

The guy that invented water skis is from Lake City. Tried 'em out on Lake Pepin. The Birthplace of Water-skiing, the Chamber of Commerce calls it. They get an argument from some place in Florida, though..."

He lost track of what the driver was saying.

"...Lake City is another slow place for trucks. Thankfully only two sets of lights. Not too bad." Then motioning to his left, he continued. "See that place, Wild Wings? They are one of the biggest publishers of wildlife art in the world. So big that it took them over a year to realize that a bookkeeper had embezzled a quarter of a million dollars."

He didn't say anything. He was getting drowsy. Random thoughts about the trip. Irene's ranch, his mother, the fugitive Mal, LaDonna Mae, and Montoya passed through his mind. From time to time the truck driver's voice intruded on his reverie.

"...got so damned constipated, I sat on the can for an hour.... John Catlan painted these bluffs back in the early 1800's..... named the place for Chief Wabasha.....See Grumpy Old Men? Took place here. Ice fishing. Ever try it? Gotta be nuts to sit out in the cold trying to catch mercury contaminated fish....Come through here in the Fall and there'll be thousands of swans over there. Weaver Bottoms. Call them Tundra Swans now. Used to be called Whistling Swans. Why the name change, I don't know. There's Bass Camp. Fishing must be big. Always a lot of boats here. Fishing rigs cost twenty-five, maybe thirty thousand dollars. Fish locators. GPS units. Underwater TV cameras. Two hundred horse-power motors. Trolling motors. More electronics than a shuttle flight....Little town of Rolling Stone. They tried to get the Rolling Stones to visit once, but they never did. Might yet. They're still going strong in their dotage...."

As they passed the exit ramp for Minnesota City, Lleyellyn realized with relief that they were almost to Winona.

"....Goodview here is separate from Winona, but they both

look like one town to me. Can't tell where one ends and the other begins," the driver said. "I'm going to drop some of these vehicles at Walz Buick on Third Street. That far enough for you?"

"That'll be fine," he said, relieved.

The driver continued his non-stop soliloquy as they passed ShopKo and the HyVee store and stopped for a signal light in the left turn lane for Gilmore Street near the Starling Motel.

"Just a few more blocks," Lleyellyn thought.

They proceeded past Winona State University and stopped for another red light at Broadway.

"Just three or four more blocks."

He was aware the driver was looking at him as they waited for the light to change.

"Sorry. What did you say?" Lleyellyn said, wondering if he may have missed something important.

"I've enjoyed talking to you. Tell me about yourself," the driver said.

When the light changed to green, and they pulled ahead. Lleyellyn said, "Well, I'm in town to tie up a few loose ends."

They turned right on Third Street, proceeded a half block, and stopped next to the automobile dealership.

"Well, here we are. Wish you would of told me more about yourself, buddy boy, but it was sure good talking to you. Now, about that fifty you owe me."

He opened the door, handed the driver the money, grabbed his pack and jumped down to the pavement.

"Learned a lot. Thanks for the ride."

oOo

Winona didn't look any different. He had only been gone a couple weeks. The town was the same, but he felt like a stranger. But he had changed. His long hair was gone. No more black pants and jacket. No one would recognize him, he was sure of it. He hadn't looked this clean-cut since the sixth grade.

He was wearing blue jeans, a yellow tee shirt and a Green Bay Packers ball cap. No one would give him a second glance.

He walked across the street to the Prime Cake and Steak Restaurant, sat at the counter, and picked up a folded newspaper someone had left behind. It was the Winona Daily News.

MANHUNT CONTINUES, the headline read in bold, black type. Under the headline the paper read, *Continued on page 8.*

Lleyellyn turned to page eight. The article was brief. The sheriff assured the public that the search was continuing. It was concentrated in the Mississippi backwaters where the suspect grew up. Most disturbing to him was an indication that manpower was being scaled back until more solid leads developed.

They're giving up, he thought to himself.

As soon as he finished his meal, he paid, then walked two blocks toward the river to get a room at the Riverport Inn.

"I'd like a single room for at least two nights," he told the clerk.

"We've got one facing the Mississippi, non-smoking. Ninety two per night."

"Anything cheaper?" he asked.

"I can give you one facing the parking lot. Seventy-five. Includes continental breakfast."

"That'll do," he said, reaching for his wallet and removing four fifties. "I'll pay in advance."

"Can I see your credit card?" the clerk said.

"No. I'll pay in cash."

"I heard what you said. But I need a credit card for any extras. Long distance calls. Pay per view television. Breakage."

"I'm sorry," he said. "I don't have a credit card. But I can pay cash. Maybe leave a little deposit."

"I'd like to help you. My boss requires a credit card before booking a room. Nothing I can do," the clerk said before being interrupted by the telephone. "Riverport Inn. How can I be of service?"

He didn't want anyone to know who he was and that he was even in Winona. He turned and left while the clerk was still on the phone.

Of course he was familiar with Winona. He had been almost everywhere in town and he knew where the seedier motels were although he had never stayed in any of them.

He threw his pack over his shoulder and started back down Gilmore Street toward Highway 61 and the bluffs. The Vacancy sign was glowing a feeble red-orange twenty minutes later when he walked across the parking lot at the Starling Motel and stepped into the office.

The office was empty. A hand printed sign on the counter read *"Ring Bell 4 Service."* Before he could press the button, a hefty woman in a blue housecoat stepped out of a back room exhaling smoke from her mouth and nose and flicking ash from her cigarette on the floor.

"You looking for a room? This is the place."

"Yes, Ma'am," he said. "I don't have a credit card, but I've got cash money."

"You're speaking my language, Bud. Twenty-nine fifty a night. Cash up-front. Plus a ten dollar key deposit."

He removed two twenties from his wallet and handed them to the clerk.

"Sign this card," she said putting a registration card in front of him and handing him a ballpoint.

"You get the deposit back when you turn in the key."

He took the pen, looked at the card, and quickly wrote in a made up name, and address.

"John Smith, Scranton, Pennsylvania, huh?" the clerk said. "You're the fourth or fifth John Smith we've had here in the last week or two."

The clerk didn't seem to care what name he wrote.

"What kinda car you driving?" she asked. "You left that blank."

"No car. I came in by bus," he said.

The clerk didn't say anything, as she put the registration card in a metal box and turned to pick a room key from the board on the wall behind the desk.

"I can give you a room here near the office. Or there's a couple in the back."

"The back," he said. "Say, if I need to stay a couple nights longer is that a problem?"

"You've gotta be kidding. Just let me know in the morning. Still gotta pay for the night in advance."

"Okay, thanks," he said. Then thinking that maybe Montoya might already be in town looking for a room, he added, "I'm looking for a guy. About fifty. Looks Mexican. No accent. Likes to wear khaki shirts and pants. Cowboy boots. And a wide brimmed hat. Same color as the rest of his outfit. Have you seen him?"

The clerk stared at him for a moment, handed him change, and drummed the fingers of her right hand on the counter as she riffled through the metal registration box with her left.

"I haven't seen him and I'm here six days a week. No names that look Mexican in the box," she said. "If he comes in shall I tell him John Smith is here?" she added, giving him a mischievous smile.

"That's okay. I was just wondering."

"This guy you're looking for got a name?" the clerk said.

He didn't want to give her Montoya's name, so he said, "No. I just know what he looks like. Met him on the bus. Seemed to be an interesting guy."

As he pocketed the room key and picked up his pack, the clerk said, "I like to keep it quiet around here after eleven. Turn the sound down on the TV. Enjoy your stay."

Room 14 was next to last at the far end of a long row of identical aqua-colored doors. He had to wiggle the key up and down several times and pull hard on the knob before he could get the key to turn and the door unlocked. He opened the door and stepped inside. The shades were down and the room was nearly pitch black. He turned on the light and was surprised to find that the room looked clean. There was a minimum of furniture, a small TV set, an alarm clock and a picture of giant sunflowers on the wall above the bed.

He placed his pack on the floor and opened the door to the bathroom. It was small. There was a shower, basin and toilet. He removed the paper strip across the toilet seat and took off the plastic wrapper on a plastic cup. He took a drink of water, used the toilet, then removed his boots and stretched out on the bed.

CHAPTER TWELVE

May 25

Yesterday he had traveled for twenty hours, maybe longer. He'd lost count. He had fallen asleep as soon as his head hit the pillow. He didn't realize he had been sleeping until he heard a knock. It sounded like someone was knocking on his door with the point of a room key. He thought it was housekeeping. He sat up and walked to the door. He was surprised to see that there was a peek hole in the door. He looked out and could just make out the top of someone's head with jet black hair. He was convinced it was the maid.

The safety chain was missing. He hadn't even noticed it before. He slowly opened the door.

Looking back at him was Montoya. Lleyellyn stepped back, and Montoya entered the room.

"Clerk told me you were looking for me," Montoya said. "Sent me down here to see Mr. Smith."

"Well, I described you to her, but I didn't give any name. Said I met you on the bus."

"Good thinking. How'd you get here so fast?" Montoya said.

"Heck. I didn't know how long it would take you to get here. I was going to try and find you."

Then Lleyellyn continued, "I hitched a ride with several different truckers. Irene's idea." After a pause, he added, "How'd you find me?"

Montoya pulled the chair back from the small table next to the television, turned it around, and sat down. Shay closed the door and sat on the bed. They faced each other.

Lleyellyn wouldn't have recognized Montoya on the street. He was wearing Levi's, a dark blue polo shirt and a Twins baseball cap. He had on a pair of black Nikes.

Montoya broke the brief silence.

"I know why you're here. Irene means well. I intend to be back in Montana before I'm missed."

"Well, she asked me to come look for you. Doesn't want you to do anything you'll regret. That'll put you back in prison."

They continued looking at each other. He wasn't sure what else to say at first, but then decided to get to the point.

"Irene figured you came back here to track down Mal for killing my mom. Is that right? You never met her. You hardly know me."

Montoya stood up, walked over to the window, parted the blinds and looked out. Seemingly satisfied, he turned and faced Lleyellyn.

"There's some things that just don't seem right. Some things I feel I have to do. The guy that assaulted Irene did it. Bragged about it. Joked. Jury found him not guilty. It wasn't fair. It wasn't right. It wasn't just. I did what had to be done. My conscience is clear. There is a right and there is a wrong, you know."

He nodded that he understood.

"I can see that. You knew Irene. You knew her attacker. I don't understand why you feel so strong about my mom."

Montoya removed the cap, ran his hands through his hair, sat back down in the chair, and then looked intently at him.

"Well, I felt it was hitting close to home. Irene brought you home to her place. Gave you a job. You learned about the murder there at the ranch. It just seemed that it was something close –

not a stranger deal. It just hit me that it was someone getting away with murder. I figured I could help straighten things out."

"You're willing to risk going back to prison for someone you never even met?"

Montoya gestured by turning both palms up.

He doesn't understand why he's doing it either, he thought.

"I promised Irene I'd try and get you back before you do something you'll regret."

"I've never done anything I've regretted," Montoya said, then added, "Yet."

Lleyellyn believed him and wondered what else he'd done along the same vein.

"At least can you call Irene? Tell her that nothing's happened."

Montoya shook his head, stood, parted the curtains and looked out the window again.

"Look here, we're both in Winona. They haven't caught him yet, have they?"

"The paper says they are still looking for him. But they're using fewer officers," Shay said.

Montoya took a cell phone out of his shirt pocket.

"Call that detective you talked to before. He won't be able to tell where the call's coming from. See if there's any later news."

He did as Montoya suggested. He heard the detective answer on the second ring. He learned that they were still looking for Mal.

"We're still looking. We've adjusted personnel resources," the detective explained.

"You mean you're cutting back the number of people involved?"

"I think he's holed up in the river bottoms where he grew up. We'll find him. It's just a matter of time."

He wasn't reassured, but he thanked the detective, disconnected the call, and handed the phone back to Montoya.

"No, they still haven't found him. Fewer searchers though. Personnel readjustment, he called it." Then he added, "Want to call Irene?"

Montoya took the phone, folded it closed, and returned it to his shirt pocket.

"I think we should do a little investigating of our own. See if we can come up with something that will help lead us to him."

"How? I mean, what can we do? I don't know where he is."

Montoya told Lleyellyn his ideas. He listened to them carefully.

When Montoya was finished explaining, Lleyellyn said, "I guess it's worth a try."

Montoya never did say how he had tracked him down at the motel.

When they left the motel room, Montoya pointed out a beige Ford Taurus. They got in and Montoya explained that he had a friend rent the car in Missoula. No one could trace the car to Montoya as long as the friend kept his mouth shut.

"I trust him," Montoya said. "We were at Granite City together, and I helped him out. He owes me."

Shay directed Montoya to his mother's house. They drove slowly past it. There was blaze-orange crime scene tape across the front steps. Mal's pickup was in the yard. One of the front tires was flat.

They circled the block and drove by the house a second time. No one was outside along the entire block. Montoya drove down the back alley and Shay got out next to the bushes near the detached single-car garage.

"We'll meet back at the motel," Montoya whispered, before he drove away.

Hidden by an untrimmed hedge and the backyard fence, Lleyellyn snuck up to the back door. It was locked, but the key was in its usual place over the sill.

Slowly he opened the door and entered the building. The smell of rotting food assailed his nostrils. It was almost over-powering. Swallowing back the urge to vomit, he edged his way inside. He tried not to breathe unnecessarily. Then he gave an involuntary shudder when he saw a dried puddle of blood on the kitchen floor. Myriad flies were buzzing around the room.

Forcing himself to continue, he entered his mother's room. He was looking for any clue as to where Mal may have gone.

The bed was unmade. The sheets and blankets were piled in the corner under an overturned chair. He put the pile on the bed to see if there was anything under it. He saw some clothes and a single black tennis shoe that he recognized as his mother's, but nothing helpful.

Several louvers in the closet door were broken. He didn't know if the damage was recent. He opened the closet door. A few garments were hanging on wire hangers and more were on the floor. He picked up the clothes from the floor and put them in the pile on the bed and added the ones on hangers. There were several folded tee shirts in a stack on the single shelf and two boxes. One was labeled Kotex; beneath it was a cigar box. Lleyellyn took down the Kotex box. It was unopened. He placed it on the bed. He was hopeful that the cigar box might contain something useful and was disappointed when he picked it up and discovered it was empty

Quite a few items were haphazardly lined up on the floor of the closet. In addition to several pairs of women's shoes, there was a small red vacuum cleaner and a stack of a half dozen cardboard shoe boxes. He picked up the stack and placed them on the bed. He made a place for himself and sat down to look through them. He could tell by their feel they weren't empty.

He was disappointed to find only shoes in the first two boxes. The third box contained the mate to the unmatched tennis shoe he had noticed earlier. The last box seemed different. When he removed the lid he discovered a bundle of letters. Some were from his grandparents to his mother. Others looked like Christmas cards. He noticed one from his mother's old boss and a couple of others from a college. He didn't take time to read them, but he took the cigar box from the shelf and put the items he wanted to keep inside. Then he discovered that the last box was nested inside a top from another shoe box. He lifted the box off of this inverted extra top and discovered some things he had never seen before.

The first was a photograph of his mother holding a baby and standing with an older couple and a beaming man in an army uniform who was about her age. He turned the picture over. He recognized his mother's small neat handwriting. *"Me with Llyn. (age four months) Ma, Dad and Ernie,"* she had written in pencil.

Lleyellyn held the picture up to catch more light. He had never seen the picture before. He knew his father had been killed in an accident at work. He didn't know his father had even had a chance to see him after he was born. He wondered what other secrets his mother had managed to keep.

There were several other pictures in the box. One was a picture of him taken with his kindergarten class and Miss Luedtke, his first teacher. Another was a picture of his mother with long hair. He thought it might be her graduation picture. Then he found copies of his mother's birth certificate and his. On the very bottom was a picture of Mal and his mother on their wedding day under a white arch that said *Little Chapel of Flowers, Reno, Nevada.* His mother looked happy. So did Mal. He realized that he had never seen Mal look so happy in real life.

What he had discovered was interesting, but he knew it was

no help in finding Mal.

Everything in the closet was his mother's. He realized that Mal must have kept his own stuff somewhere else.

The top of the dresser on the back porch was Mal's. The room was cluttered. Empty beer cans, several over-flowing ashtrays, mis-matched socks, a handful of pennies and a near-empty toothpaste tube and other junk. It was all Mal's.

He had a hard time opening the drawers because the supporting hardware was broken. He didn't see anything but clothes, most were filthy. When he rummaged around in the clothes in the bottom drawer he felt something on the very bottom. It was a book. He picked it up from under some tee shirts. It was a scrapbook. In neat script it said, *Our Son.*

The first page of the book revealed that it had been prepared by Mal's mother and had been presented to him when he graduated from high school. *To Our Son Malverne,* an inscription read. *You will go far in life, love always, Mom and Dad.*

Lleyellyn had never thought much about Mal's past and had never heard anything about his parents.

He thumbed through the scrapbook and noticed a series of pictures taken when Mal was growing up. The last page held a photograph of him in an army uniform wearing a green beret.

He closed the book and took it and the cigar box with his mother's pictures and papers back out to the kitchen.

As he was about to sit down at the table, he noticed someone walking their dog pause in front of the house while the dog sniffed around. He remained silent and out of sight until they were gone.

He carefully looked through the rest of the house and didn't find anything that appeared useful.

He took the book and the box with him as he left the house through the back door. He placed them on the back steps. He wanted to inspect Mal's pickup before leaving.

He slowly crept along the house toward the front, keeping out of sight behind bushes, making sure no one was walking by until he was between the front steps and the truck. He eased the passenger door open. Someone had obviously been through the cab. The door to the glove compartment was hanging open. It was empty. The stereo had been removed, only some protruding wires were left hanging from the dash.

Under the seat he found nothing but trash, old beer cans, discarded Copenhagen containers and fast food wrappers.

In the bed of the truck, Mal's old tackle box had been broken open and most of the contents removed. There were two or three red and white bobbers and several plastic worms scattered about. In the half-opened bottom drawer of the tackle box he found some stained, crinkled up papers. He took them out. They were folded up maps that had gotten wet, then dried out. He took them, returned to the back of the house, picked up the cigar box and scrapbook and left the yard. As far as he could tell, no one had seen him either coming or going.

It took Lleyellyn a half hour to walk to the Starling Motel. Montoya's rental car was not in the lot. It was a little past noon.

Once in the room, he put the things he had taken from home on the bedside table and looked them over carefully.

He examined each of the pictures that had been in his mother's shoe box before turning his attention to Mal's scrapbook he had found in the dresser.

It was obvious that Mal's mother had kept a careful chronological record. There was a copy of the birth announcement from the Winona Daily News and a card from the Community Memorial Hospital with the new baby's footprint. Then there were photographs of Mal with his parents and grandparents and several of him with a dog that looked like a blue heeler or similar breed.

He came across of picture of Mal and his kindergarten class and his first grade report card. *"Deportment: excellent."*

On the following pages snapshots taken in the country or on vacations showed Mal with his family. Several pictures showed Mal with friends in a flat-bottomed fishing boat. Over the years, Mal got progressively taller, but pictures of the same boat appeared again and again. There were pictures of Mal holding stringers of fish kneeling by the same boat and others with him standing next to an eight-point buck, entering an ice fishing shanty, and of him sitting on a rock. In the background of a majority of the pictures he recognized a local landmark, Trempealeau Mountain.

It was clear to him that Mal had grown up near the Trempealeau region of the Mississippi River. Then with an insight that suddenly snapped into focus, he realized that he knew where Mal must be hiding.

He thumbed through the final pages of the scrapbook. The last page showed Mal in uniform. It looked like his graduation picture from Ranger school.

He's hiding near Trempealeau Mountain, he thought. *That damned mountain is in as many pictures as Mal is. He was raised near that mountain. He's gotta be holed up there somewhere.*

Shay found a telephone book in the top dresser drawer. There was a map of the Mississippi River and the area around Winona. Trempealeau Mountain was shown on the map.

It looked like Trempealeau Mountain was undeveloped. Next to it, and a part of Wisconsin, was Perrot State Park and just to the north was the federal Trempealeau Wildlife Refuge. The map didn't show any symbols for roads, trails or camp sites on the mountain. It was uninhabited. He saw that the mountain looked like it had once been completely surrounded by water, but now it was connected to the Wisconsin side of the river by railroad tracks which cut across a bend in the river and skirted the southwest side of the mountain. The only way to reach the mountain by land was by crossing a railroad trestle.

Damn! he thought. *Mal's gotta be on that mountain. I'd bet on it.*

oOo

He was reading the letters he had found in his mother's shoe box when he heard a knock on the door and let Montoya in.

"I think I know where he's hiding,"

"Okay. Good. How'd you find out?" Montoya said.

He explained what he had found, showed Montoya the photographs and the map.

"Good work. Sure seems logical. He's been around that mountain all his life. Strange the way it's situated. Almost a no-man's land."

Montoya sat on the edge of the bed and thumbed through the pages of the scrapbook. He held the last page up so they could both see it.

"Army-trained. He'll know how to attack and defend himself. Any ideas?"

Lleyellyn studied the picture. Then he looked at Montoya, trying to read what he was thinking.

He's not giving anything away, Lleyellyn thought. *I don't know what he's got on his mind.*

"Maybe I should call the cops. Tell them what I found. And what I think it means," he said.

Montoya didn't reply. He got up and filled a glass from the faucet at the sink in the bathroom.

Then he took a drink, deep in thought. Finally he sat down on the bed again and looked at Lleyellyn.

"I think you might be on the right track. But it's only a hunch. Too early to go to the cops," Montoya said.

"What do you think I should do, then?"

"Let's get out of this place. The clerk can put the two of us together. Put your backpack in the car. We'll find somewhere to spend the night. I'll tell you what I think on the way."

They got in the car and Montoya headed south on highway sixty-one.

"When you were checking out your Mom's house, I did some checking myself at the library and checked around some other places. The cops think he's hiding out in the Mississippi River backwaters. They told you that. It's in the paper. I found some maps and had some copies made. I also drove down river to La Crosse and back to Winona on the Wisconsin side. I saw Trempealeau Mountain but I didn't give it much thought at the time. Except it isn't much of a mountain by Montana standards."

Four or five miles south of Winona, Trempealeau Mountain came into view.

"That's it over there," Shay said.

Montoya drove past the mountain, crossed over the median separating the north and south lanes and reversed direction. He parked at a vista point directly across from the mountain.

"That's Trempealeau Mountain on the left," Lleyellyn said. "Next to it on the right is Brady's Bluff. In Perrot State Park. See that shelter building near the top? Our class hiked up there in the fifth grade on a field trip."

Montoya opened the glove compartment and took out several sheets of white copy paper. He leafed through several pages, then showed one to him.

"Here's the detail showing Trempealeau Mountain," he said, before they got out of the car and stood looking across the river toward the bluffs..

They both looked at the map together, glancing at the mountain from time to time.

"See how the railroad tracks cut across here and connect to the island?" Montoya said pointing at the map.

"It looks like it's part of Perrot State Park, but it isn't. The DNR controls it. Nothing on the map shows improvements, campsites, that sort of stuff. Looks completely undeveloped."

"The only way to get to the mountain is by the railroad tracks... or by boat," Lleyellyn said. "They told us on the school trip Trempealeau means 'foot in the water' in French, according to the teacher."

They got back in the car and turned back to the southeast at the first cross-over on the divided roadway. As they headed toward La Crosse, Wisconsin along the Mississippi bluffs on the Minnesota side of the river, Montoya outlined his plan.

"I'm going to get a motel room in La Crosse for us. I have a borrowed ID I can use so I won't have to use my name. When we get ready, we'll go scout around, see if we can get a handle on where your stepfather's hiding."

oOo

Shay waited in the car while Montoya entered the lobby of the Super 8 Motel. He came out in a few minutes and they drove around to the side, took their belongings out of the trunk, and entered the motel by a rear door.

There were two double beds in the room. The air conditioner was on and it was comfortable. Montoya threw his suitcase on the nearest bed and nodded toward the other one for Lleyellyn to take. Then he took the sheaf of photocopied maps he had taken from the car and aligned them on his bed so that the entire area around Perrot State Bark, Trempealeau Mountain, the wildlife refuge and the adjoining river bottoms was laid out before them.

"I've been thinking," Montoya said. "Here's what I think we should do."

Montoya went over the details of his plan. Lleyellyn listened carefully. When Montoya finished, he said, "Makes sense. If we find him I just want to hand him over to the cops. Or tell the cops where he's at. Okay?"

Montoya stepped back and looked at him before replying.

"Whatever you say. We've gotta see if we can find him first."

Then before he could say anything else, Montoya opened his suitcase and started to unpack.

While he was doing this Shay had to use the bathroom. When he came out Montoya had placed his gear neatly on the desk.

Next to a pile of carefully folded clothes were two small caliber automatic pistols, two identical cell phones, a roll of duct tape, a pair of binoculars, two pair of rubber kitchen gloves, and several flashlights. Lleyellyn was caught off guard. He had been unaware of Montoya's preparations. Montoya had been planning things very carefully for some time. *He wants to get started tonight; not wait until tomorrow*, he realized.

"Do you need all this stuff?" he said. "What if you get stopped with the guns?"

"You mean we. Not just me," Montoya said, giving him a serious look. "We can't capture a killer without weapons. These guns can't be traced. The small one is a thirty-two. It's for you. I'll take the thirty-eight. We won't use the guns unless we have to. You have my word on that."

Lleyellyn knew Mal would be armed. He didn't know if he would be able to use a gun himself.

"I'm not sure I know how to use one of those things," he said, pointing to the automatics.

Montoya picked up one of the guns and handed it to Lleyellyn, butt end first, and then reached for the other one.

"They both operate exactly the same. Look. Just pull back here," Montoya said, using the other pistol to demonstrate. "Now it's cocked and ready to go. Pull the trigger and it'll shoot automatically ten times after you pull the slide back for the first shot."

He looked at the gun in his hand. He wasn't sure if it was loaded or not.

"It's not loaded, don't worry," Montoya said. "Now pull back the slide."

He did and heard it click into the cocked position.

"Okay. Now pull the trigger."

He did as he was instructed. He heard the sound of the hammer striking the empty chamber.

"Good. If the gun was fully loaded, it would keep on firing every time you squeeze the trigger. There's nine shots in the clip. With one in the chamber there's ten altogether. The old ads used to say *'Ten Shots Quick! Savage Automatic.'* Been around for decades. Cheap. Reliable."

"They almost look like cap pistols," Lleyellyn said after studying the weapon in his hand and comparing it to Montoya's. "They're so little."

"Not toys," Montoya said. "They'll do nicely for close work, believe me." Then picking up one of the cell phones in one hand and a flashlight in the other, he said, "You know how to operate these, right?"

"Yes," he said, before realizing that Montoya was making a joke. "I'm an expert with a flashlight. Can make do with a cell phone, too."

"I've got the number of the cell phones taped to the back. One says 'A' and the other says 'B.' We can check in with each other. These work better than those little walkie-talkies you can get at Wal-Mart. We'll be able to keep in communication at all times."

They decided to rest until late in the afternoon so they would be able to keep out of sight better.

Lleyellyn woke up when he heard the water running in the

bathroom. When he sat up he realized it was raining outside and starting to get dark.

"The rain will help," Montoya said as he came into the room. "Shouldn't be anyone hiking around when we get there."

Montoya pointed out his share of the gear and they both put on the black nylon windbreakers Montoya supplied.

He watched as Montoya put a pistol in his belt and Lleyellyn did the same thing with the other one. They both put a handful of cartridges in a pocket of their jackets and zipped the pockets shut. They loaded up the rest of the gear and went out to the car.

"We won't be coming back," Montoya said. "Wait here while I make sure we didn't leave anything behind."

Shay waited in the passenger seat until Montoya came back out.

"Looks clean," he said. "I don't want to be traced back here."

He didn't reply as Montoya started the car and pulled out of the parking lot and headed north.

"There's something else I want to do," Montoya said, as he turned left at a Kwik Trip station and drove into a parking lot near a medical clinic just off I-90.

"I'm looking for a Ford Taurus, white, looks like this one," Montoya said as they slowly drove between the rows of parked cars in the parking lot of the Gundersen Lutheran Medical Center.

"There's one." Shay said as they were about to pass a white car to his right.

"No. That's a Merc," Montoya said. "There has to be a lot of Tauruses around, though."

They found one near the back of the lot when they started down the next row.

"Great. That one's better than what I was looking for," Montoya said. "Before we stop look around at the light poles.

See if you can spot any closed circuit TV cameras."

They spotted two cameras trained on the clinic entrance but none covering the far reaches of the vast parking lot.

Montoya pulled into an empty space two cars beyond a white Taurus.

"It's got an Arizona license plate. Did you see that?" Montoya asked.

"Yeah. What difference does that make?"

"Arizona cars only have one license plate for the rear end. Twice as easy as removing two separate plates," Montoya said taking a screwdriver out of the glove box and getting out of the car. "Keep an eye out. Let me know if anyone's coming. This will only take a minute."

He was quickly back in the car, the Arizona license plate in his hand. Handing it to Lleyellyn, he said, "Okay. Let's roll."

Montoya drove north from La Crosse, never exceeding the speed limit. They turned off on the road to Perrot State Park. When they came to a parking area next to a fruit stand closed for the day, Montoya pulled in and removed both license plates and affixed the Arizona plate on the rear of the car.

They followed Highway Thirty-five to the City of Trempealeau, passed the Trempealeau Hotel, and turned right at another sign pointing to the park and followed a two-lane road that followed along the banks of the Mississippi River.

The rain had slackened off but the darkening sky looked ominous. They passed the unmanned ranger kiosk at the entrance to the park. A sign indicated that there was a mandatory fee for anyone parking in the park.

Montoya pulled the car into a small parking lot used by hikers. The other six spaces were empty. A sign warned that cars without state park permits displayed on the windshield would be ticketed. The rain continued at a steady drizzle. Through the trees they could see a string of barges being pushed up river. The railroad tracks were at the bottom of a steep drop off in front of them.

Montoya reached behind the passenger seat and picked up a plastic bag. "I bought these rubbers to put over our shoes. Don't want to leave traceable footprints. Something else I learned at Granite City."

They took a minute to put the rubbers on. Lleyellyn watched as Montoya slipped on a pair of rubber gloves, and then did the same. They wiped off each of the guns and their clips with a hand towel Montoya had taken from the motel room.

Montoya handed him the box of 32 caliber shells and told him to wipe off each shell as he inserted them in the clip. Montoya did the same with the thirty-eight.

"Okay. Let's get started," Montoya said, opening the door and getting out of the car.

Lleyellyn knew what he had to do. Montoya's instructions had been clear. He watched Montoya pat his pockets to make sure he had all his gear. Then, after flashing a tight smile at him, Montoya followed a path down to the tracks. He stepped across the first set of double tracks and then looked back up to him. Montoya signaled for Lleyellyn to start moving, then Montoya turned to his right and started walking between the two sets of tracks in the direction of Trempealeau Mountain, which was out of sight around a curve.

While Montoya walked between the tracks, Shay followed the paved road. The plan was for him to find a place out of sight of anyone watching from the mountain to where he could observe the railroad trestle connecting the east end of the mountain with the park.

When a car passed by, he hid behind a tree. Montoya had stressed how important it was that no one be able to place them in the vicinity.

Shay rounded a curve in the road. The trestle came into

view below him to his left. He kept his eyes on the tracks until he saw Montoya crossing the trestle.

He continued on, surreptitiously making his way down the embankment from the road to the railroad tracks. Just before he reached the bottom of the embankment, the lights of a locomotive came into view from the direction Montoya had taken. The engine had been slowing down before it reached the trestle. As soon as the engine crossed the trestle it pulled onto the parallel tracks of the siding which ran between the mainline and the river.

It took several minutes for the slowing train to come to a complete stop. The last car crossed over the trestle and was clear of the main line before coming to a halt.

He could hear intermittent ticking from the cooling brakes of the freight cars and saw the dim regular flashing of the light on the rear of the last car.

It was obvious to him that if Mal was keeping a lookout on the trestle he would have seen Montoya crossing over. Shay was confident that he himself had stayed out of Mal's sight when he moved into his present position. He had kept well concealed in the brush and trees.

Shay stayed among bushes and tall grass as he made his way carefully to the near end of the trestle. He had remained invisible from the mountain.

Lleyellyn peered out between leaf-covered branches. He could see from his end of the trestle to the other side. Montoya was out of sight.

Across the trestle the railroad tracks curved to the left along a tree-lined berm. Trempealeau Mountain was around the curve. He could see the top of the mountain, but the base was hidden by trees along the water's edge.

Lleyellyn eased forward until he was a few feet from the main line track as it crossed the trestle. A small ditch cedar provided cover. From this vantage point his head was level with the tracks, giving him an unobstructed view. Anyone stepping on the trestle would be instantly in sight.

The plan was for Montoya to circle the base of the mountain moving generally counter clock-wise. He would walk out in the open making no attempt to hide. Their hope was that Mal would see Montoya and think he was alone. They didn't know how Mal would react if he spotted Montoya, but they thought they might flush him out so he would start moving.

Maintaining his vigil, Lleyellyn checked his gear. It wasn't completely dark. He had the cell phone in his shirt pocket with the sound turned off. If Montoya called he would feel it vibrate.

He felt his pocket to make sure it was still there. He took the pistol out of his belt. The rubber gloves weren't a bother. He pulled back the receiver and cocked the automatic. He hoped he wouldn't have to use it.

Lleyellyn placed the gun on a flat cross member about waist high on the side of the trestle. He heard a train whistle in the distance and thought a train might be approaching before he realized it was coming from across on the other side of the river.

He had been instructed not to leave his vantage spot until Montoya told him to. They had estimated it would take Montoya up to an hour to circle the base of the mountain. He wasn't sure how long he would have to wait for instructions.

The rain had slowed to a light drizzle and he thought it would make waiting a little less uncomfortable, but then it started up again, harder than ever. He didn't feel the phone start to vibrate at first because of the steady rain drops bouncing off his jacket. When he took the phone out of his pocket it slipped out of his gloved hand, but he managed to catch it before it hit the ground.

Everything was drenched. The phone was slippery. He fumbled the phone open, paused, took a breath and said, "B, here," identifying himself the way Montoya had instructed.

"It's A," Montoya said. "Followed the tracks to the far side. Starting around the back now. Seen nothing so far. Out."

He wasn't sure if he was supposed to reply or not.

"Okay," he said.

It had taken Montoya about twenty minutes to get to the far side, much faster than they had estimated. *Should know if his plan works pretty soon.*

He kept watching the trestle. He heard two or three cars hiss by on the wet roadway above and saw a houseboat heading slowly upstream on the Mississippi. There was no movement on the trestle.

He was thinking about the things that had happened since he left Winona less than two weeks before, and about LaDonna Mae and the ranch, when he was jarred out of his reverie by the vibrating phone.

"Hi!" he said and almost added "It's Lleyellyn," but he stopped himself and simply added, "B here."

"A. Think I saw him. Got him moving. He might be headed your way. Got it?"

"Okay. Yes. Got it," he managed to say.

He realized that Montoya had hung up. He closed his phone and put it next to the gun on the cross member. He took a careful look across the trestle, then picked up the gun. He didn't see anybody, but he wanted to be ready just in case.

The rain made everything slippery. He put his hands back in his pockets to dry the gloves off. All he could hear were drops hitting his jacket and the steady background noise of the falling rain.

The phone started moving. It was vibrating again. He reached for it. It skittered out of his reach, skidded down the side of the gravel railroad bed, and plopped into the water below.

"Shit!" he said quietly to himself. *Montoya had something to tell me. Maybe Mal's moving this way.*

In the distance he heard the faint sound of another train whistle, then almost at the same time he saw movement across the trestle.

Lleyellyn carefully held the pistol making sure it didn't slip out of his hands and into the water. Looking across the trestle he could see someone starting to cross. It wasn't Montoya. Too tall. As the person came closer, he saw camouflage clothing. The guy had a full beard he didn't recognize, but he hadn't forgotten the familiar walk. It was Mal.

Mal stopped in the middle of the trestle and looked back over his shoulder. Again Lleyellyn heard the sound of a train whistle. It seemed closer this time.

Mal started walking across the trestle toward him.

Lleyellyn remained dead still, hidden behind the side of the trestle. He held his breath. Mal would see him if he stopped and looked over the side.

Crouching even lower, he heard muffled footsteps approaching on the wet timbers. He looked up as Mal passed him.

"Stop right there!" he said. "Turn around."

Mal stopped, slowly turned, recognizing his stepson.

"You little cocksucker," he said, "what're you gonna do with that cap gun?"

Lleyellyn held the pistol with both hands pointed at Mal who was standing between the rails of the closest set of tracks.

They stood there for a brief moment looking at each other. He didn't say anything. Mal held his hands at his sides balled into fists.

Lleyellyn was startled when he heard another train whistle. Mal didn't seem to bat an eye. A train was approaching from the south.

He motioned with the gun for Mal to move off the tacks.

They could clearly hear the train rumbling toward them,

the sound reverberating off the cars of the train stopped on the siding.

The lights on the front of the engine came into view as it rounded a curve, then the whistle blew.

Despite the noise and the obvious danger, Mal never took his eyes off him and he didn't flinch or react in any visible way as the train came closer.

Lleyellyn hid the gun behind his back with his right hand so it wouldn't be seen from the engine.

He could barely hear when Mal shouted, "Looks like your buddy's gonna get caught on the bridge."

He glanced over his shoulder, catching a glimpse of Montoya waiting at the far end of the trestle.

He turned back to keep an eye on Mal. Lleyellyn was going to give the engineer a wave, trying not to arouse curiosity.

As the train bore down and almost reached them, Mal made a dash to cross the tracks and get away. Lleyellyn hesitated, but before he could even point the gun, Mal slipped on the loose gravel, and plunged head first in front of the train.

Shay stepped back from the passing engine. He couldn't see what happened to Mal. The train was going too fast and the noise it made was nearly overwhelming. He was aware that something was bouncing along the side of the tracks. He turned back just in time to see that it was a boot. Mal's boot. It was slowly rotating as if in slow-motion. He realized a foot was still inside it. He watched with horror, his mouth wide-open, as it bumped along the ground, skidded down the embankment, then bounced into the water beneath the trestle.

He looked back at the spot where Mal had fallen. He could see a shape between the tracks but the steady stream of the fast moving steel wheels made it difficult to see.

Mal's dead, he thought. *Has to be.*

It seemed to take forever for all the cars of the rapidly

moving train to pass. The train didn't slow down. He realized the train crew never saw a thing.

When the train finally passed, the sound lingered for several long seconds. He couldn't bring himself to look at the rounded shape between the tracks.

Montoya came running up to him, glancing toward the tracks where the shape of Mal was laying between the rails.

"Saw the whole thing," Montoya said. "Son-of-a-bitch tried to make a run for it. Saw him slip and fall. Stupid fucker."

Lleyellyn didn't want to look any closer.

"He's dead, isn't he?"

Montoya walked up onto the roadbed and took a closer look.

"Shit! No! Fucker's moving."

Lleyellyn scrambled up the bank and stood next to Montoya.

Mal sat up, oblivious to his injured leg. He looked at Lleyellyn, fumbling with the pocket of his down jacket.

Montoya aimed his pistol at Mal. Lleyellyn, following his lead, did the same.

"Keep your hands in sight!" Shay yelled.

Mal hesitated for a second.

"How much money did that stupid cunt mother of yours…" he was saying as he started to pull something out of his jacket pocket.

Lleyellyn's gun went off before he realized he had pulled the trigger, followed immediately by two quick shots from Montoya.

Mal was thrown back, but he was still moving his hands. Montoya took a step forward, reached down with his right hand, and fired a shot point-blank into his forehead.

"He's dead now. Out of his fuckin' misery."

Lleyellyn stood there in shock. Montoya took the gun from

his hand and put it in his own pocket.

"Grab his legs," Montoya said. "We've got to move the body."

Lleyellyn was slow to react.

Montoya grabbed Mal by the shoulders.

Lleyellyn remained motionless.

"Okay. Now, grab that leg!" Montoya shouted.

Lleyellyn did as he was told and helped carry the body off the tracks. Following Montoya's direction, they moved it to the adjoining siding.

Montoya placed Mal's upper body on the nearest rail of the siding directly in front of the last pair of wheels of the final box car of the train waiting on the siding. He motioned Lleyellyn away, then positioned Mal's legs so his body was lying prone and spread-eagled on the track.

"Trying to obliterate the gunshot wounds," Montoya said.

Lleyellyn still hadn't said a word when they heard the train on the siding begin to move, a sound moving from car to car as slack was taken up and the train started to roll forward.

When the box car had moved and the train was on its way, Montoya said they had to move the body away from the tracks so the crew on the next train wouldn't see it and call it in. He ordered Lleyellyn to help him drag Mal's severed body across the tracks.

He followed Montoya's instructions in a daze, oblivious to the brain matter, blood and excrement on and around the rail, and helped hide Mal's body in the weeds, between the siding and the river.

Montoya walked over to where Lleyellyn was standing and put his hands on his shoulders.

The rain started to fall harder, diluting the gore and washing off the rails and the surrounding ties and aggregate.

"Let's get out of here. There's nothing more we can do

now," Montoya said.

He didn't reply. He stood looking first at Montoya, then at the place where the body had been placed on the track. He was disoriented. The sound of Mal's head exploding as the steel wheels passed over it reverberated in his ears. He hadn't heard it at first, but the sound was there now. A delayed reaction.

Montoya gave Lleyellyn a small shake and looked at him until their eyes met.

"Lleyellyn! Let's go," he said. "Got all your gear?"

Lleyellyn made an effort to pull himself together.

"I dropped the phone when you called the last time. It slid down in the water," he said, pointing to the place where he had last seen it.

Montoya walked over to where he had pointed. The cellphone was lying in the water partly submerged.

"You're in luck. It's right here on the edge," he said, picking it up.

Mal's boot was floating nearby, trailing a cloud of blood on the surface of the water.

"Let's get back to the car before another train comes along or somebody spots the body," Montoya said. "That rain's cleaned up the scene pretty good. If it keeps raining, so much the better."

Lleyellyn followed Montoya up the path. Montoya fished the keys out his pocket and opened the trunk. They placed their gear, including the guns and cell phones in a box, and Lleyellyn slammed the lid shut.

When they were seated in the car Montoya removed first the rubber gloves and then the rubbers on his feet and Shay did the same. They placed them behind the front seat.

Montoya looked at him as he started the engine.

"How you doing?"

He gave a slight shake of the head. The fresh images and sounds were imprinted on his mind.

"I don't know what to think. I can't believe it, really."

As he backed the car out of the parking space, Montoya said, "It was a dumb thing for him to do. Stupid. He didn't want to get captured. He was reaching for a weapon. We had no choice. He just didn't make it."

He was silent as Montoya switched on the headlights and headed out of the park. As they passed the empty ranger ticket shack he noticed a wet yellow piece of paper stuck behind the wiper blade.

"Is that a ticket?"

"Must be. Some guy from Arizona didn't pay the parking fee," Montoya said, flashing a brief smile at him. Then he turned on the wipers and the ticket, saturated with water from the rain, disintegrated.

As they were passing the Trempealeau Hotel, Lleyellyn said, "Do you think he was trying to commit suicide?"

Montoya didn't say anything at first. Then he said, "We don't know what he was thinking. We never will." Then after a pause he added, "It must have been suicide."

As they continued south toward La Crosse and the interstate, Montoya told him that they would be back in Montana in a day and a half, maybe two.

"No one will know we were gone," he said.

Montoya slowed down and pulled off the road at a public boat landing on the Black River. He parked near the boat ramp. The lot was deserted. It was still raining, the lot was wet and several pot holes were overflowing.

"We're gonna get rid of the guns and stuff," Montoya said.

They took the box out of the trunk and walked to the water's edge. Together they threw the cell phones and the guns out into the current.

"I guess we can keep these flashlights," Montoya said. "But let's check in the car to see if there's anything else we should get rid of now."

They used the flashlights to check in and around the car. Montoya took the two pair of rubbers out of the car while Shay was rummaging through his pack.

When he joined Montoya at the water's edge, Montoya was trying to stretch one of the rubbers over a rock. "When we throw these in, I want them to stay sunk," he said.

Lleyellyn put what he was carrying down and helped Montoya weight the other rubbers and the rubber gloves before they threw them in the river. Then he picked up Mal's scrapbook and threw it out into the stream. It floated a few yards downstream, quickly became water-logged, and sank.

They picked up the other things they had set on the ground. Lleyellyn held the box with his mother's letters and the picture of his father. He looked at it for a few seconds, removed the birth certificates, then he threw it into the water as well. They walked back to the car without either one saying anything.

As he was buckling his seat belt, Montoya stopped.

"One more thing. I forgot the plates."

He got out, removed the Arizona license plate from the back end of the car and reinstalled the original Montana plates, front and rear. He tossed the Arizona plate in the river and got back in the car.

Before pulling back on the road he stopped, and turned toward Lleyellyn.

"It's not my business, really," he said. "But tell me, why did you throw that box of your mother's things in the river?"

He gave Montoya a serious look, the light from the instrument panel making him appear older than his eighteen years.

"I've got my secrets," he said. "I figure my mother's got hers."

He thought Montoya was going to say something, but he didn't. He put the car in gear and pulled out onto the highway.

CHAPTER THIRTEEN

May 26

Jeremy and Bobby parked their bikes on the side of the road, grabbed their fishing poles and a can of night crawlers, and made their way down to the rail road tracks.

The pool under the trestle was usually a good place for sunnies, occasional catfish, and once in a great while a northern pike.

Bobby was the first to get his hook baited. He adjusted the red and white bobber about eight feet from the hook and plopped the rig in the water.

Jeremy was just getting ready to toss in his hook when Bobby shouted.

"Holy shit! There's a boot with a foot still in it!"

Jeremy took a look at the boot.

They ran up to the road, jumped on their bikes and peddled as fast as they could to the park ranger's shack at the entrance to Perrot State Park.

They managed to blurt out to the ranger what they had seen.

oOo

Jim Cole had been a park ranger for seventeen years, the last seven at Perrot. Nothing surprised him. He had seen it all performing his official duties.

He drove to a spot directly above the railroad trestle, activated his law enforcement flashers, and followed the trail to the place the boys had described.

Sure enough, the boot was where the boys told him it was. He could see flesh protruding from the top of the boot around the severed ends of two round bones.

Cole was experienced enough not to disturb the accident scene.

He went back to his vehicle to call the Trempealeau County Sheriff's Office in Whitehall, Wisconsin on his car radio.

"Park Ranger Cole here. Perrot State Park. Investigator Good Thunder, please."

Cole told the investigator what the two kids had told him and what he had found.

"Looks like something for your office," Cole said.

"Does, doesn't it?" Good Thunder said. "Wait there, should be there in twenty, maybe twenty-five minutes."

oOo

While Cole was waiting for the sheriff's investigator to arrive, a south-bound came around the bend and started across the trestle. As it came closer he saw five crows and a turkey vulture rise up from the far side of the tracks.

He knew immediately where the rest of the body would be found. The scavengers were at it already.

oOo

Good Thunder arrived with a deputy. They shook hands all around.

"The foot's down there," Cole said, pointing. "I bet the

rest of the body's over there by that dead cottonwood. I haven't looked, but I saw several crows and a buzzard fly up when the last train came by. Carrion of some kind got their attention."

oOo

They located the body and called the county coroner.

The coroner was an insurance agent from Holmen. He had been a corpsman in the Navy and had been elected to the post of coroner. He ran unopposed. By most accounts he did an adequate job.

When the coroner arrived, Good Thunder and the assisting deputy showed him the three parts of the body.

The coroner was careful not to get too close to avoid compromising evidence. He took several photographs from a distance.

"Put the parts in three separate bags. Get them up to the medical examiner in Hastings. I'll give her a call, a heads up as to what we're sending up there. The body's been run over by a train, but I can't imagine how it scattered itself the way it did without help."

"Good call," Good Thunder said. "We need an autopsy, that's for sure. Thanks for getting here so fast."

oOo

Before bagging up the body parts, Good Thunder and his deputy carefully surveyed the scene and took crime scene photos. The rain had diluted the blood and scavengers of some kind had disturbed the flesh and tissue lying on the railroad bed.

Good Thunder was able to conclude that the body had been run over head to anus by a train moving southbound on the siding. It had occurred on the easterly of the pair of tracks of the siding. Brain matter, blood, bits of viscera and excrement still adhered to the sides of the rail and eight or nine inches out from each side of this rail on the ties and gravel. The same pattern of bodily residue repeated itself in the same order two yards to the south where the wheels of the rail car had deposited some of the gore as the train moved along.

He pointed out what he had seen to the deputy who took several close-up photos.

"The spatters of blood and shit don't go far. Train was going slow when it ran over the body," Good Thunder said.

They continued their methodical search of the scene. The deputy noted traces of blood on several ties on the main line. They both closely examined the area and saw traces of blood up to a yard from the easterly most rail on the mainline.

"What's your take on this?" Good Thunder asked the deputy.

"Probably blood that was spattered when the foot was severed. The spatters seem to be going in a northerly direction and out a lot farther from the rail than those over on the siding. Plus the foot was over there, a good thirty-five, forty feet to the north from here. Must have been hit by a north bound train going pretty fast."

Good Thunder didn't say anything, but he did nod his agreement and gave an appreciative smile to the deputy.

They continued scouring the scene. The deputy found a shell casing wedged between a roadbed rock and a railroad tie. He retrieved it with forceps, and placed it in an evidence bag. Good Thunder recognized it as a casing from a thirty eight.

Good Thunder examined the ground looking for footprints. He saw what he was certain were the sneaker prints of the two boys that discovered the foot, and faint hatch marks made by rubber over shoes. He made plaster casts of them all.

oOo

The next day Good Thunder contacted the boys who had found the foot. He compared the soles of their tennis shoes to the plaster casts of what he had suspected were their shoes. His suspicion was confirmed when he found exact matches.

oOo

He didn't know if the plaster casts he had made of the cross hatch pattern he suspected were made by rubber overshoes had anything to do with the death.

He confirmed by an internet search that there were rubbers with a similar pattern widely available. They were sold by Wal-Mart and several other retailers.

CHAPTER FOURTEEN

May 27

The first thing the medical examiner and her assistant did when they took the three body bags out of the cooler was x-ray each bag separately.

One of the x-rays of the part of the body to which the right arm was attached revealed a thirty-two caliber bullet imbedded in the shoulder.

The body had been so extremely mangled that virtually all of the jaw and teeth were either missing or pulverized. Dental records would be of virtually no help in identifying the body.

There was one intact eye. Brown.

The clothing and boots were carefully removed.

The two boots were a matched pair. Size eleven wide.

A tattoo was found on the left bicep. The faded words *Born to Be Bad* appeared on a banner across the front of a dagger.

The clothing from both halves of the body was confirmed to be from the same garments.

There was a billfold in the inside pocket of the cammo-colored down jacket. The wallet contained forty-seven dollars in U. S. currency, a Minnesota Driver's License in the name of Malverne Lester Dotwich, and a Minnesota Fishing license, expired, bearing the same name.

In the right hand pocket of the jacket was a nine millimeter Sig Sauer automatic pistol with a full clip and a round in the chamber. Strapped to the right calf was a scabbard holding an Army combat knife.

oOo

Good Thunder returned a call to the medical examiner after he got back from lunch.

"First, let me summarize. All three parts are from the same body. Identified as Malverne Lester Dotwich. I assume you have the spelling. Winona address. Minnesota."

She went on to explain what she had found.

"You want a cause of death. Can't give you one right now. He had a foot severed in one incident. Was shot in the shoulder in another. Neither of those things killed him. He was run over from head to tail. That trauma destroyed a lot of tissue. Don't know if he was dead when run over that second time or not."

"Gun shot is interesting," Good Thunder said. "We found a shell casing. Thirty-eight caliber."

The medical examiner paused before replying.

"The bullet we removed from the shoulder was a thirty-two caliber. Think he was shot more than once?"

"Beats me," Good Thunder said. "Would explain a lot, though, wouldn't it?"

oOo

Good Thunder received another call just before his shift ended.

"Ralph, this is Jim Cole at the park. Something I thought you should know. I issued a ticket for non-payment of the park entry fee on the night of the twenty-fifth. 2045 hours. Light colored, maybe off-white Ford Taurus. Had an Arizona plate. I placed the ticket under the wiper. Didn't write down the VIN. Raining like a son of a bitch at the time.

"Most people just drop the fee and fine in the box on the way out of the park. This one didn't.

"Car was at the east Brady's Bluff trailhead parking area, maybe 400 yards from the crime scene. Only car there at the time. Thought you might be interested."

"Track down the owner?" Good Thunder asked.

"Checked out the registration for the plate with the Arizona DMV. Plate reported stolen. Car was stopped by an Onalaska patrolman near Valley View Mall. Old guy driving. had stopped at the Gundersen-Lutheran walk-in clinic. Wife needed help with her oxygen. Driver didn't know the plate was missing. Officer remembered the driver. Ex-military. Former United pilot. Traveling from Scottsdale to their summer place in Door County. Clean record. Officer remembered there were two of those *Support Our Troops* decals on the back of the car and a big red University of Wisconsin *W*. The car I ticketed had no stickers."

"Know the model year?"

"No. Not really. Those damned Tauruses all look alike to me. Wasn't the one with the oval rear window, though, I remember that."

oOo

He picked up the phone on the second ring.

"Winona County Sheriff's Office. Williams speaking."

"It's Ralph Good Thunder. Found something you'll be interested in."

"Heard some talk about the body you found on the tracks. That it?"

"Right. Your guy. Malverne Lester Dotwich. Identified

by his DL and fishing license which were in his pocket. Also a tattoo. *Born to Be Bad.* Left bicep. Saw it on your wanted posting."

"Well, that's good news. Killed his wife. Been looking for him. He's been on the run," Williams said. "Wonder how he was so stupid enough to get run over by a damned old train, as David Allen Coe would say. Remember him?"

Good Thunder didn't reply at first.

"You don't even call me darlin,' darlin,'" he finally said. "How could I forget the perfect country and western song?"

Then Good Thunder got back to business.

"I just got through talking to the medical examiner. She can't give me a cause of death. Too much trauma to the body. She did say he was run over twice by trains and shot in the right shoulder just before he died. Can't tell if he was shot anywhere else."

"Interesting. She know what kind of bullet?" Williams said.

"Thirty-two. Pistol. Ballistics hasn't looked at it yet," Good Thunder said, then added, "When we searched the scene we found a bullet casing for a thirty-eight."

"Find anything else?"

"Took a plaster cast of marks left by a pair of rubbers, you know, overshoes. Common kind. Can buy them anywhere. Nothing else to see except the messy leakage from the body. Rained a lot so most of it was washed away. Scavengers and other varmints were there, I'm sure. We did a thorough search. I'll send you my report."

"Ends my manhunt," Williams said. "You looking for his killer?"

"Got any ideas?"

oOo

The next morning Ralph Good Thunder took a call from the M. E.

"Good Thunder," he said.

"Hi! Rosalie calling from the medical examiner's office. About your case. Malverne Lester Dotwich."

"Nice to hear from you.

"There were fragments of teeth, dental fillings and such that showed up when we looked closer at the x-rays. We extracted the metal fragments and sent them to the forensics lab for analysis. Just got the results."

"Anything I need to know?"

"Some of the fragments were from dental fillings, but others were bullet fragments. No intact bullets. Just small pieces. Pretty flattened out. Distorted. Lab says they were bullet particles. Couldn't give any ballistic opinions. Caliber, source and so forth, unknown. Couldn't tell me if they were from a thirty-two or a thirty-eight or whatever."

"Doesn't help too much. Don't know if our thirty-eight casing means anything. But sure makes you wonder." Good Thunder said. "These fragments, where from exactly? The head?"

"Think so. Basically, because some of the bullet fragments were sort of fused to pieces of dental fillings. Must of happened when the wheels ran over them. Best they could do."

oOo

Good Thunder had arranged a lunch meeting with Investigator Williams at the Prime Cake and Steak in Winona. Being from adjoining jurisdictions, they had worked together in the past.

After ordering and their preliminary chit chat was out of the way, Good Thunder told Williams about the ballistic report he received from the medical examiner.

"Sure seems he was shot and then put on the track," Williams said. "What's your take on it?"

"I agree. My sheriff wants to wrap this up. Close the file. A murderer gets run over and killed by a train. No good leads. No public uproar. Wants to just leave it as an accidental death."

"Well, my boss seems to be thinking along the same lines. Our murder is solved. The killer's dead. Dotwich's death is not in his jurisdiction. Our official book is closed," Williams said.

Their orders came and they ate in silence.

"Got any ideas who might have shot him?" Good Thunder said.

Williams took a long sip of his iced tea and considered the question.

"You and I both know family and close friends are the most logical suspects. Far as I can tell, he had no real friends and was pretty much a complete loner. Of course, there's his stepson. He was close to his mother. Trouble is, he's working on a ranch in Montana. Probably still there."

They both agreed there were some loose ends that needed to be tidied up, even if their bosses were happy with the way things were. They each decided to make inquiries on their own time.

"I'll check up on the son. Name's Lleyellyn Shay," Williams said.

"Let me know what you find out. I'll try and find out what trains were through during the time frame when it happened, talk to the engineers and the rest of the train crews."

They concluded their meeting by agreeing to meet again for lunch when they had something to discuss.

"Let's make it on my side of the river," Good Thunder said. "How about Beedle's in Centerville?"

"That'll work for me."

oOo

Ralph Good Thunder talked to the Burlington Northern Santa Fe Railway trainmaster in La Crosse, from where he was referred up the chain of command to an official in Chicago.

He was on the phone for an hour and a half, but he learned a lot.

Anytime a suspected body is seen by the engineer or any crew member, the train is required to stop. Local law enforcement is notified immediately, then a call is made to the railroad.

There had been no such report for the time period in question in the sector between Bluff Siding, Wisconsin and Winona, Minnesota, the stretch that included the siding south of the Trempealeau Mountain trestle.

Every BNSF lead engine was equipped with a video camera which showed the track ahead of the engine at all times.

The video recordings of all incidents were retained by the railroad and delivered to the National Transportation Administration investigators assigned to the incident. Copies were retained for potential litigation. The tapes were on a continuous loop. If no incidents were video recorded, the tapes were automatically recorded over every three or four hours. The railroad official told Good Thunder that no incidents had been reported and that any tapes made during the time frame in question had been recorded over at least once.

During the twenty-four hour period in which Dotwich could have had been killed, Good Thunder learned that there had been twenty-six north-bound trains passing through on the main line and twenty-three heading south. Four of the south-bound trains had pulled onto the siding south of the trestle during the same period, but no north bound trains.

At Good Thunder's request, the railroad official agreed to fax him the names, addresses, and phone numbers for the train crews for the four trains that had used the siding and the same information for the forty-nine trains that had passed through on the main line.

He received a fax with the names and other information for the trains that had used the siding within an hour. He saw all the crew members were based in La Crosse and lived between Tomah, Wisconsin and St. Charles, Minnesota.

Forty-five minutes later a second fax arrived with similar information for the crews of the other trains, both engineers and conductors. Some ninety in all. The crews were regularly dispatched either from the Twin Cities or from La Crosse.

CHAPTER FIFTEEN

May 31

It took three work days for Ralph Good Thunder to reach all of the crew members on the two lists he had been sent by the railroad.

Only one remembered seeing anyone near the trestle. He arranged to meet with that engineer, D. D. Banifl, at his home in Hokah, Minnesota that evening.

oOo

"Not much to tell you. I was heading north, well, really northwest at that point, to St. Paul. Near the trestle, just before you get to Trempealeau Mountain, I noticed two guys standing by the side of the track. East side. They were moving a little ways away from the track when I got a call from headquarters. I didn't pay any more attention to the two guys. Passed on my way without incident. Arrived in St. Paul right on schedule."

"What did these two guys look like?"

"Just two guys. Dressed like duck hunters or fishermen. Blaze orange or cammo. Not sure. One had his back to me. The other one gave me a wave. Didn't think anything about it. I remember it because you don't see a whole lot a people in that area, but it happens."

"Height? Build? Anything?" Good Thunder said.

"Not really. One guy might have been bigger. That's about all."

"See any fishing poles, anything like that?"

"Don't recall. Don't think so."

"Guy was run over right there. Think you could have done it?"

"Shit no!"

"Why do you think you remember as much as you did?"

"That's easy. That was my first trip after I got back from Iraq. Recall the whole damn trip pretty good. For a time I didn't think I would make it back."

"What was the call from headquarters you got about? Remember?"

"Sure. My boss calling to welcome me back home. Thanked me for my service to our country."

oOo

Irene picked up the phone in the kitchen.

"Hello!"

"Irene Boyd?" Investigator Williams said.

"Yes, this is she."

"This is Investigator Williams in Winona, Minnesota."

"Yes. You are the one investigating the death of Lleyellyn's mother. Isn't that right?"

"Yes, Ma'am. May I speak to Mr. Shay?"

"He's outside working today. I can have him call you back."

"Would you?" Williams said and gave her the call back number. "Have him call me collect."

Irene thought the call was over, but then Williams continued speaking.

"Can I ask you a few questions?"

Irene paused before responding.

"Sure. What about?"

"I just need some background. How long has Mr. Shay worked for you?"

"It's been about two weeks, now. Gave him a ride after the end of rodeo week in Miles City. I needed some help on my outfit and he didn't have a job."

"Does he have a car?"

"No. He was hitchhiking when I met him. Know he doesn't have a driver's license yet, either."

"What kind of work does he do for you?"

"Helps around the ranch. Fixes fence. Unloads supplies. There's a movie company fixin' to film a picture here. He keeps an eye out for me. Makes sure they don't go where they aren't supposed to. Doing a real good job, too."

"He have any friends there?"

"There's just me and my foreman. Lleyellyn has a friend from the rodeo. Kid named Tole. Moved back to Wisconsin. They keep in touch by phone, I think. Don't know if they write."

"Tole's last name?"

"Winters. Tole Winters."

Irene remembered LaDonna Mae in town, but decided not to mention her.

"Has he been gone from the ranch at all since you hired him?" William said.

"Oh, no. We're nearly two and a half hours from town. Hundred miles, give or take. There's a post office in the back of a store twenty miles up the road at Crow Wing. Population's about six. He's never been there. He's been here all the time. No place to go really."

"Any other employees there?"

"Just Mr. Montoya. He's my foreman. Of course, the movie crew's starting to arrive. They'll have at least a hundred here when the cattle are unloaded."

"Can I talk to your foreman?"

"He's out somewhere. I'll have him call you."

oOo

Irene waved to Montoya when she saw him and Mully cross the yard. He walked over, Mully running ahead so she could scratch her ears.

"Mr. Montoya, the investigator at the Winona, Minnesota sheriff's office wants you to call him. Has some questions about Lleyellyn."

Montoya looked at her, his face remaining expressionless as usual.

"He asked me if Lleyellyn had been away from the ranch. I told him no. Probably wants to ask you the same stuff."

He placed the call and was put through to Williams.

"Manuel Montoya here. You asked me to call."

"Yes, sir. I did. Thanks for getting back so quick."

Montoya could hear papers being shuffled.

"You are the supervisor of Lleyellyn Shay?"

"I am the foreman here at the ranch where he works."

"How long as he worked for you?"

"Couple weeks. Ever since Miss Boyd hired him and brought him to the ranch."

"What's he do for you?"

"Whatever we need. Cleaned up the storage building. Rode the fence. About twenty miles worth. Made repairs as needed. Helps us keep an eye on the movie crew, shows them where to set up their tents and park their rigs and stuff. Has done a good job, so far."

"Has he left the place at all since he got there?"

"No. He's been here every day. And night."

"Mr. Montoya, have you yourself been there the entire time

since he was hired?"

Montoya paused before he answered. He was certain the investigator had checked his background before calling.

"No, I haven't. Did spend one night in town. I'll admit to you I'm on parole. I have to let my agent know if I'm gone overnight, get permission. Can't leave the state of Montana. I'm not about to screw up and end up back in prison. Really had no infractions since I was paroled. Plan to keep it that way."

"I can verify that. Thanks for being so forthright."

Montoya thought the call was about over but Williams had one more thing he wanted to know.

"Give me the name and number for your parole agent."

oOo

"Corrections," the receptionist answered after the first ring.

"I'd like to speak with Agent Cramer. This is Sheriff Investigator Williams."

"Maggie," agent Cremer said by way of greeting and introduction.

Williams explained who he was and what he wanted.

"Manuel Montoya. He is my client. Has been for about five months, ever since his previous agent retired. He has been a model parolee. Never missed an appointment. No violations. Maintained steady employment. Paid off his restitution. Probably recommend him for early discharge next year."

"Has he been gone for any three, four day period?"

"No. Can't leave the state. Interstate compact. I don't see him every day, but I certainly have no reason to suspect he's been gone. Irene Boyd, his employer, would let me know, I'm sure, if he ever absconded. He's given me no reason whatsoever to suspect any violations of any of the terms of his release. Wish all my clients were like him."

oOo

"Lleyellyn, this is Investigator Williams. Hope I'm not too early."

"No. That's fine. No problem, I was going to return your call in a few minutes anyway."

"I've got some news for you. Your stepfather's body was found and has been identified. He was hit by a train near Perrot State Park and Trempealeau Mountain."

Lleyellyn didn't respond.

"Are you still there?" Williams said.

"Yes, sir. I can't believe it. How could that happen?" After a pause, he added, "I'm glad you found him, glad he's dead. I could probably come back there, now. If I wanted to. Right?"

Williams was going to express his sympathy for the whole situation, but the line went dead. He wasn't sure if the connection was lost or if the other party hung up.

CHAPTER SIXTEEN

June 3

A Winona County Sheriff's squad car was parked in front of Beedles when Good Thunder pulled in next to it.

They got down to business right away while waiting for their orders.

"Talked to Shay's boss in Montana. She picked him up hitch-hiking near Miles City, Montana. Hired him as a helper around her ranch. Said he never left the ranch since he got there. Apparently never went into town. Never away overnight."

Williams turned a page in his notebook.

"Foreman named Montoya verified Shay never left the place. He's interesting. Montoya. Volunteered to me he's on parole. Talked to his agent. He's been a model parolee. Can't leave the state. She expects him to receive an early discharge."

"What was his crime?" Good Thunder asked.

"Checked it out. First degree assault. Incarcerated in Sioux Falls, South Dakota. Spent about eighteen years in the slammer."

"Learn anything else?" Good Thunder said.

"He, that's Shay, met a guy his age from Wisconsin on the train. Tole Winters. Rodeo cowboy. Winters has talked to Shay by phone. Nothing much there, but I will follow up and talk to this Winters kid, face to face."

"I checked out the railroad people," Good Thunder said. "Narrowed it down to the train crews that passed the area during our time frame. The crews on the trains using that siding saw nothing. One engineer on the main line heading north sort of remembers seeing two guys near the trestle. Nothing suspicious. Was distracted by a call from his headquarters at the time and forgot about them."

"Two guys there," Williams said. "That's something."

"Yeah. They have closed circuit TV cameras on the front of each engine. Never watch the tape unless there's an incident. No accidents reported in that sector. Tapes automatically recycle and get recorded over."

"Great," Williams said. "Anything else?"

"I had our intern contact bus companies, train station, air ports and rental car places near Miles City to see if the names of Shay or Montoya appeared anywhere. They didn't."

Their daily specials arrived. The hot roast beef sandwiches with mashed potatoes and gravy tasted as good as they looked.

When they were done, Williams said, "Can we agree to close the files?"

oOo

Tole was making the last few rounds on the John Deere riding mower at his uncle's place when a squad car pulled into the yard and parked next to the house.

The driver's side door of the squad car opened and a tall man in a tan uniform stepped out.

It was an out-of-state car. The license plate was from Minnesota and instead of a number it read *SHERIFF. Winona County* was stenciled on the side. *We Aim to Serve.*

The deputy got out of his car and looked toward the mower. He had one loose end he wanted to tie up.

Tole stopped the mower next to the officer and shut off the motor.

"I'm Investigator Williams," the deputy said. "I'm looking for Tolland Merriweather Winters. That you?"

"Yes, sir. People call me Tole."

The deputy moved closer. The cast on Tole's right arm held in place by a sling made a normal handshake impossible. Williams touched the brim of his hat instead.

"I'm from Winona County. Cross the river. Know where it is?"

"Been there a few times. Considered going to Winona State for a while. Maybe St. Mary's," Tole said.

"I'm investigating a homicide up our way. You know Lleyellyn Shay?"

"Sure. I met him when I was going out to Montana. We were riding Amtrak together. Told me he's from Winona. I also know his mother was killed by his stepdad. He called and told me about it. We're good friends."

"How well do you know him?"

"I was heading out west to enter a rodeo in Miles City. That's in Montana. I had a seat on the train. Had my saddle and everything with me. He and I started talking and hit it off. Said to call him 'Lou Ellen,' said everyone else did. He was planning to go to Portland or Seattle or somewhere to look for a job. Said he had to get away from his stepfather. Guy was a drunk. Abusive. Beat his mother. He was scared of him. Said his mother told him to get out. Away from his stepfather."

Tole noticed a cord leading to a recording device clipped to William's shoulder somehow. He knew their conversation was being recorded.

"Look, Mr. Williams, Lleyellyn and I hit it off right from the beginning."

Tole got up from the mower and stood facing the investigator.

"We got off the train together and got a ride to Miles City.

Shared a room at a motel. When I was at the rodeo he found a job working at the rodeo beer tent. When I fucked up my shoulder after getting throwed, he took me to the doctor and helped me out until I decided to come back here."

The deputy was jotting down something in a notebook. Tole couldn't read anything in Williams' look.

"I trusted him. Still do. I decided after getting busted up that I was done with rodeo. Came back here. Told Lleyellyn to keep my association saddle. Sell it. Worth a few bucks."

"What kind of saddle?" the deputy asked.

"Association saddle. For riding bucking horses. Special rig. Small. No good for anything else."

Tole wondered why the investigator was asking questions about his friend.

"Why so interested in Lleyellyn?" he asked. "I have his address if you want to contact him. Phone number, too."

"I know where he is. Talked to him a couple times. I'm just doing routine background stuff.

"When is the last time you've heard from him?"

"I haven't seen him since I left Montana. He called me once to tell me his mother died. Murdered. And I got a letter from him a few days ago. He sent me a check for $950. Sold my saddle. Some guy working on a movie they're making at the ranch where he works bought it. Was a fair price. I haven't even had a chance to cash the check yet."

"He write anything?"

"Said he lucked out. Some stunt man on the movie crew saw the card he posted in the mess hall and bought it."

"I'd like to take a look at the note and the check. And the envelope it came in. You still got them?"

"Think so. Let me go find them."

The deputy started to follow but was interrupted by a call on his radio.

Tole went in the house and up to his room. The letter with Lleyellyn's check was on the dresser.

He removed the note and looked at the check. Drawn on the Wells Fargo Bank in Miles City, the bank he and Lleyellyn had gone to when they opened their accounts when they first got there.

Then he picked up the envelope. Addressed to Tole Winters. The return address said *L. F. Shay, c/o Irene Boyd, Boyd Ranch, Rt. 2, Box 17, Crow Wing, MT.*

The postmark was faint. He brought it closer. He could barely make out the words Hudson WI and the date. May 24th.

Tole went back outside as Williams was finishing up his radio call.

"Here's the check," he said and handed it to the deputy. Then he handed him the note.

"Couldn't find the envelope. Must have tossed it. Sorry about that."

Williams read the note and scrutinized the check. He made some notes in his pad.

"Know if this check is good?" he asked.

"I figure it is. Lou Ellen is an honest guy. He found my billfold on the train and returned it to me before we even got to know each other. Nothing was missing. I had nearly two grand in there. And I know he had a bank account. We both opened up accounts at the same time when we first got to Miles City."

"Where'd you toss the envelope?"

"I don't remember," Tole said, looking the investigator in the eye. "Probably in the kitchen after I opened my mail."

"Let's check that trash can."

"Won't do any good. Burned the trash yesterday," Tole said. "Can I check?"

"Sure. I guess so. If you want. My uncle's not back yet."

Tole showed the deputy where the kitchen garbage can

was and also led him upstairs so he could check the wastepaper baskets in his room and in the bathroom. The only thing he found was the empty tube from a roll of toilet paper in the bathroom and a used coffee filter in the kitchen.

Before he left, the investigator looked at Tole.

"Son, did you see the post mark on the envelope?"

"No sir, Mr. Williams. Sure didn't. Never even looked at it."

When the officer got in his car and turned onto the county road, Tole pulled the envelope out of his back pocket and walked behind the house to the trash barrel. He lit the envelope afire. It burned slowly, curled up and turned to ash.

This book was printed in Tucson, Arizona
by AlphaGraphics Commercial Printing Services

www.tucsoncps.com